S0-AEL-202

A Form of Death

a&b

A Form of Death

Roy Lewis

First published in Great Britain in 2000 by
Allison & Busby Limited
Suite 111, Bon Marche Centre
241-251 Ferndale Road
Brixton, London SW9 8BJ
http://www.allisonandbusby.ltd.uk
Reprinted 2001

A catalogue record for this book is available from the British Library

ISBN 0 7490 0482 7

Printed and bound in Spain by
Liberdúplex, s. l. Barcelona

An answer is always a form of death.
John Fowles, *The Magus*

Prologue

His hotel room in Bukit Bintang gave him a view over the gas station. Open for twenty-four hours, it was a convenient picking-up point for prostitutes and transvestites. He had availed himself of neither. His preferences lay elsewhere, and opportunities to indulge his own personal tastes were numerous across the northern border, in Thailand. He also had an affection for Sri Lanka. Prices were so reasonable there.

He was sweating, in spite of the air conditioning of his room. The hotel was one of the oldest in Kuala Lumpur but had recently been refurbished, and the foreign exchange rates had made it a target for tourists seeking comfort and modem conveniences at a low rate. It suited him: he sought the anonymity of a drifting tourist population.

He was sweating because he was nervous. Crossing the borders always caused a certain jangling of nerves because of the mandatory death penalties his activity carried—although the authorities normally fought shy of carrying out the penalties on Westerners. This time it was more serious: it was a year or more since he'd done the run and somehow he felt that there was a different air about the whole thing. The passport check had been longer than usual; a customs officer had drifted past nonchalantly stroking a moustache and studiously avoiding his eye; and in the journey from the airport there had been a car that seemed to maintain a discreet distance from his own hired airport limousine.

But it was just imagination, he guessed. The unfamiliarity of the run, the difference in the arrangements, and Cullen's insistence that he make the presentation a personal one. The contact on the phone had been equally surprised: there had been a long hesitation, a mumbled discussion with a muffled handset, and then a curt agreement.

Nine o'clock. The time was fixed. The meeting would be brief. He'd still have plenty of time to get to KL International Airport for the midnight flight back to England. And once aboard his worries would be over. He was clean, carrying nothing—a twelve-hour flight in business class where he could relax, have a few drinks, and savour memories of some of the sexual adventures he'd enjoyed in Thailand these last two weeks. Not strictly part of the assignment, but everyone was entitled to a certain relaxation, especially when dealing with dangerous people, and the smooth-limbed young boys needed the money anyway.

He packed his flight bag: he always travelled light, consigning nothing to the hold. He made his way down to the reception area on the first floor and paid his bill in cash. Credit cards could be traced. In the street outside the air hit him in a humid, hot surge. There would be rain soon, he guessed, and it would then get cooler but at the moment the crowded, colourfully lit street—streamers and red lanterns celebrating Chinese New Year and Hari Raya Aidilfitri—was bustling sweatily in a mingling of ethnic types: Indian, Chinese, Malays, red-faced Englishwomen whose large buttocks squirmed to escape too-tight shorts, lean New Zealanders, outsize Australians with backpacks, all flowing in the swirl of Bukit Bintang and spilling over towards Star Hill. It was Friday night and everyone seemed to be out and about among the cafés, restaurants and large department stores perambulating to the thud of distant rock music from a bar down the street.

He hardly needed to wait for a taxi. He was hesitating at the taxi stand when a yellow vehicle slid out from a side street and the cab driver caught his glance. He agreed to make the trip to Seramban, and then on to Kuala Lumpur International Airport. It was a good fare—metered, it could be eighty dollars or more.

The sights of the city moved past slowly as they inched their way along Bukit Bintang, into Jalan Imbi and then wove their expert way to the highway. The twin towers of KLCC—highest building in the world—glittered and gleamed with a thousand twinkling lights; the Menara Tower stood out on its hill like a gigantic lollipop, and everywhere were the paraphernalia of celebration: red banners, balls of gold, lamp-posts decked in streamers, the sidewalk trees glittering with multicoloured, dancing decorations, the streets crowded, busy, jangling with sound and colour and life. Then they were on the new motorway. A quick stop at the tollbooth and they were on their way, the city quickly receding, slipping into the darkness behind them.

The cab driver found the address without too much trouble: it was in an area of Malay housing, expensive yet government-subsidized, the house he sought protected by electronically controlled gates, neat and quiet. He was a little surprised by the lack of pretentiousness. He would have expected a more lavish, highly guarded lifestyle for a man in this dangerous business. He told the cab driver to wait, explaining that he would not be long: the man nodded, happy enough to keep the meter running.

The electronic gates were already open. Porch lights lit up the small garden brightly: a stretch of manicured lawn, bougainvillea, a sprinkling fountain, lush vegetation. He stood on the narrow porch outside the front door, dark Malaysian rubber wood, and pressed the buzzer. There was a short wait, and then the door opened. The man framed there was of medium height but powerful build. He had dark, indifferent features, a curved nose; he was perhaps southern Indian in origin. His hair was black and slick, his eyes cold with a careless hostility. Knowing the form, the visitor slipped out of his shoes and entered the house as the dark man stood aside.

He was shown down a short corridor, and into a large room with a raised area at one end. An old woman sat there: she must have been eighty years of age, and she ignored him. To his left was a small, Hari Raya decorated sitting room, furnished with deep, comfortable settees. There were two women seated there, watching television, an old Malay film whose black-and-white flickering images reminded him of Hollywood films in the Forties. One of the women was perhaps forty years of age, the other possibly twenty years younger. Both wore slacks and loose shirts; both were slim and beautiful. They glanced at him, and the older one murmured something to her companion. She rose and switched off the television. As they walked past him they both inclined their heads gravely. The older woman said, "You are expected. The Dato' will be with you shortly."

They moved towards the old woman and spoke to her briefly, then gently escorted her from the room. She walked with difficulty. They passed several large photographs on the wall beside the staircase: they depicted the same chunky, black-moustached, floridly handsome man in colourful Malay formal dress. In one photograph he was pictured with the Prime Minister; in another presenting a gift to the Yang di-Pertuan Agong; a third showed him speaking at a conference, here dressed in a smart dark business suit. A man of consequence, distinction, and contacts.

But that was what Malaysia was all about: contacts.

"Who are you?"

He started: he had not heard the soft-footed approach of the man in the photographs. The Dato' was dressed in dark slacks and white open-necked shirt. Gold glittered at his throat and wrists. His eyes were dark and appraising. He was barefoot on the cool marble tiles of the floor.

"Who am I? Is it important?"

The Dato' stared at him, and a grimness touched his mouth; then after a moment he smiled, ignored the impertinence, waved a negligent hand. "Of course not. You're right. But I am surprised. I expected someone else. A woman."

"Yes?"

There might have been an edge of nervousness to the gruff belligerence of his tone; something moved darkly in the Dato's black eyes. "Yes. A woman. It has been usual, though she has never come to me personally, not here in my own house."

"She's no longer in the business."

"A pity. She had exceptional talents. I enjoyed them. But you say she is no longer involved. And you, a stranger, are here in my house. You have met my wives. You have met my mother. And you have met me."

The visitor's tongue was suddenly dry. There was a saddened, resigned note in the Dato's tone. It made him nervous.

"Cullen insisted it was necessary," he blurted.

"Cullen. Did he, indeed?" The Dato' spoke excellent English: his accent held a slight hint of the States, though his intonations were well-bred Cambridge. But his silkiness was menacing, and the courier suddenly began to sweat again, cold runners down his back.

"Cullen asked me to make this delivery." He slid the small packet out of the pocket of his light jacket and offered it to the man in front of him.

The Dato' stared at it for several seconds, and then gestured across to the table beside the stairs. "Put it over there." He watched as the courier did as he was told, and then he said, "Cullen told you to make this a *personal* delivery?"

"Yes." He wished now it had been otherwise.

"Was there any message to go with it?"

The cool, quiet tone did not hide the controlled viciousness this man would be capable of. The courier's throat was constricted. He nodded.

"Well?"

"He…said I should tell you this is the last. It's over."

The Dato' stared at him for a little while and then a slow smile flickered across his lips. He shook his head in a mocking, wondering admiration. "The girl is no longer involved. Cullen says it is over. And a delivery is made to me personally, in my own home, in front of my wives and my mother."

"I didn't speak to them..." The words died in his throat.

The Dato's smile broadened though it was not reflected in his eyes. "No matter. Your business is done. I need detain you no longer. Thank you for the trouble you have taken. I believe you are flying back to England tonight? It's a long way to KLIA. Perhaps I could offer you the use of one of my cars?"

"I have a cab waiting outside."

"Ah. Yes. Of course. Well, I will not detain you. *Selamat jalan,* Mr…ah, but you remain anonymous. Have a good flight. And when you meet Mr Cullen..." He hesitated, then shrugged slightly. "Perhaps it is better I pass my greetings to him myself, in due time." He waved a hand. "Perhaps you would see yourself out? I have an urgent phone call to make." He was already dialling as the courier stepped outside.

On the porch, as the door closed behind him, the courier found that he was shivering slightly in spite of the warmth of the evening. He was under no illusions. The controlled, quiet tones of the man inside the house had only barely concealed a simmering anger. As for himself, he was angry too. He felt that in some strange way he had been set up. Cullen had sent him here to Seramban in a deliberate gesture of contempt towards the man in the house. The Dato' certainly saw it as an insult: it was, thought the courier, a gesture that Cullen could well live to regret.

As for himself, it was better he get out to the airport as quickly as possible. He felt vulnerable out here in the darkness, adrift in dangerous waters. The cab driver was still waiting, a wreath of tobacco smoke emerging from the open window of the cab. The courier slipped on his shoes, and hurried to the car. The driver glanced at him, flicked the cigarette in a glowing arc into the garden and sprung open the door.

"KLIA?"

"As quickly as you can."

They drove smoothly back to the highway.

Half an hour later KLIA loomed up ahead of them, a space station of an airport, all gleaming glass and steel, domed and modernist in design, airy and spacious and glittering in the velvety night. And safe. He paid off the cab driver and hurried to check in, then made his way down the elevator to immigration where a weary Malay girl barely looked at him as she ran a computer check on his documents. It was encouraging; his earlier anxieties had clearly been the result of his own paranoia, and now that he was here in the light and colour of KLIA he felt more relaxed, the tensions of the last hours ebbing away.

He moved through into the departure area, checked his flight time and then headed for the business class club lounge where he knew he'd be able to relax completely in quiet seclusion over a drink, while the time slipped away until take-off. The thought of a drink gave him pause—he might as well make some purchases in the duty free shop before he settled down. He turned, and headed past the perfumes and cosmetics into the liquor department.

He spent some twenty minutes browsing among the whiskies and cognacs before he made his selection. There was a short queue at the checkout and he fumbled in his pocket for his boarding card and passport. There was a shuffling behind him and he half turned, aware of two men in batik shirts having some sort of argument in low tones. They were Malays, and the argument seemed to be over a large pack of duty free cigarettes. He smiled—there were enough packs available to make the selection of one an unimportant matter. Even as the thought crossed his mind a warning bell rang in his head; almost simultaneously he felt the sharp jabbing pain in his thigh, like the sting of a mosquito. He swung around, but his leg was suddenly weak and he almost fell. One of the bottles he held crashed to the carpet and rolled; people stepped aside from the queue and he stood upright again, glared around, grabbing at his thigh. There was no pain now, the dispute over the cigarettes had been settled, the men had disappeared and he wondered whether it had all been imagination.

He picked up the bottle, his heart still racing, and he moved towards the check-out desk. He looked about him. Through the long windows of the dutyfree area he could see people moving along the travelator, some heading for a gate, others moving in the opposite direction back towards the departure lounge. There was a man standing beside the travellator, staring into the duty free area. He was thickset, dark, slick-haired, and there was something familiar about him but his hook-nosed features were blurring, becoming unfocused.

He blinked. When he looked again, the man was gone but he felt as though the seams of his body were coming apart, nerve ends disintegrating, a weakness drifting through his whole being. The bottles suddenly fell from his nerveless grasp. The last thing he noted in his conscious mind was the sound of a woman screaming.

Chapter one

1

He was older, of course, and somewhat greyer.

Eric Ward was still lean, reasonably fit in spite of the generally sedentary life he led as a solicitor with a small practice near the Quayside in Newcastle, just a short distance away from the Law Courts. There was no extra flesh along his jawline and his stomach was still flat and hard. But his attitudes hadn't changed either he still valued his independence, still enjoyed dealing with the underprivileged and the desperate, while at the same time being involved on his wife's behalf in the mercantile bank of Martin and Channing in London. So, overall he was much the same man as he had been when he married, ten years ago.

So perhaps it was Anne who had changed, in the manner he had feared she might, when he had first walked away from involvement with her, aware of the disparity in their ages, background and experience. He had felt then that as an ex-policeman forced to leave the force because of incipient glaucoma, and as a newly qualified solicitor with a struggling practice on Tyneside, there was an immeasurable gap between his lifestyle and hers—brought up on a landed estate, a wealthy woman in her own right when her father died, a young woman who was beautiful, accustomed to getting her own way, headstrong and determined...He had fallen in love with her, he guessed, that first time he had seen her riding down through the trees from the fell, her handsome mount picking its way carefully as the sun at her back caused her hair to flame and glow.

It all seemed a long time ago. It had been a long time ago. And yet things had worked out between them. They had married in spite of his objections and concerns; it had been a good marriage even though she had often enough expressed the desire that he should give up his mean practice on the Quayside and look after her financial interests full time. He had compromised to some extent, taking up her seat on the board of the mercantile bank, but he would not go further. It had been a continuing cause of some tension but that was something Eric Ward could not do: there was a streak of stubbornness in him, a deep-felt wish for independence, a refusal to accept that he did not need to work, with a rich woman as his wife, broad estates to manage, a county lifestyle to keep up with the aristocracy of Northumberland. Perhaps it was this that now lay at the root of his unease.

"Another drink, sir?"

The hostess in the lounge smiled at him: she was young and pretty, with burnished hair and an eagerness to please. Perhaps she was new to her job. Eric Ward shook his head. "No, I'm just waiting for my wife. I'll stick with what I've got."

The young woman glanced at the mineral water in front of him and raised an eyebrow, then nodded and turned away.

Eric laid his head back against the imitation leather seat and drummed his fingers on the chair arms. He was aware of the faint prickling at the back of his eyes—not the old cat claws that had scratched and torn at his optic nerve ends until he had almost screamed in agony, but a sign even now that in spite of the drugs he took there could still be a stirring of his old physical enemy when he felt unwelcome stress.

There was certainly a new stress in his life. He felt it, he sought its cause, he puzzled over it and yet he could not bring himself to face its reality, call for the explanation that stirred muddily in the back of his mind. He squeezed his eyes shut, trying to block out the thoughts that disturbed him and then he heard her voice as she entered the lounge, became aware of her step as she walked across towards him.

"Eric! I didn't expect to see you. I thought you were in court today."

"The hearing was postponed at the last moment. Judge Fairley was taken ill." He rose to greet her, kissing her lightly on the mouth, then gestured to the hovering hostess. "You'll have a drink?"

"Gin and tonic."

She sighed, sat down, busied herself, rummaging in her handbag for a moment. "It wasn't necessary, you know. You didn't need to be here to see me off. We'd already said our goodbyes."

He remembered them: last evening it had been almost like the old days. They had dined together in Sedleigh Hall, by candlelight, the wine had been specially chosen and they had talked easily and naturally. Later, in the bedroom they had embraced and when their lovemaking came it had been with some of the passion that had driven them at the beginning of their marriage. Perhaps that was what an impending parting resulted in—an urgent recognition of what they were in danger of losing, even briefly, through forgetfulness, or indifference. But he was not indifferent: he never had been, even though he sometimes found it difficult to express his feelings easily. He thought she understood that, but one could never tell what went on in someone else's head.

She glanced up at him, and became aware of his observation. Perhaps she realized his mind was dwelling on last night, and she flushed slightly, a smile touching her lips. She had never been beautiful in a formal way but her eyes had been wide-spaced and there was a liveliness about her that had appealed to him. Now after years of marriage he still found her attractive—more mature, her figure more rounded, but desirable, poised and elegant. The enthusiastic, girlish Anne Morcomb of ten years ago had changed into a confident, balanced, capable businesswoman...and perhaps the problem really was that it was her independence of him that he could not take.

Her drink arrived and she sipped at it gratefully. He placed his arm along the back of her chair. "What time will you be arriving in Singapore?"

She shook her head, and shrugged. "Not until about seven, I think. But the car will be waiting."

"No new developments?"

"None that I'm aware of. The California company is still insisting that they hold the timber licences as part of their purchase of Cemerlang and that our contractual arrangements are invalid. I think the whole thing is crazy, and should have been sorted out by the lawyers a long time ago. Now it has to be a series of meetings with Government officials to talk about import licences, the boards of the two subsidiaries, and the Californian legal eagles. It's all so boriing..."

"But you love it," Eric remarked, smiling.

She looked at him, and then laughed. "In a way, I suppose I do."

"Power struggles: the doughty little woman pitting herself against the big bad business tycoons."

Perhaps there was a little too much edge in his tone. She frowned. "You have your own little power struggles, Eric—though they're rather less significant than mine."

The tension he had sought to avoid was back between them. They sat silently for a few minutes, each immersed in private thoughts. After a while he called the hostess and ordered himself a whisky; Anne declined another drink. "There'll be plenty available on the long flight," she laughed, a little nervously. She glanced at his glass. "A little early for you, isn't it?"

"Time to break a habit, with my wife leaving me."

"Hardly that," she said tartly. "It's unlikely to be more than three weeks."

"With Jason Sullivan hovering like a predatory buzzard."

He had not meant to say it; he had not wanted it to come out the way it sounded. Anne glared at her drink as though it had been in some way responsible for the surge of annoyance she clearly felt. "What exactly is that supposed to mean, Eric?" she asked irritably.

"Mean? I don't know." He shrugged, sipped his drink. It burned his throat. "I don't rate Sullivan—I think he's clever, and able, but lacks balance. You already know I'm not at all happy that he's been acting as your adviser in this business—"

"Jason Sullivan, QC," she interrupted frostily, "is retained by Morcomb Enterprises as the best lawyer around in the field of corporate law. This lack of balance you talk about is really something I don't understand. What have you got against Jason? Is it his background? Or do you feel that a man of thirty-five cannot possibly have achieved legal eminence without some chicanery or dark secrets in his history?"

He was nettled: perhaps it was the reference to Sullivan's age, close to her own. "I am certainly surprised that he can find time from his intensely successful practice to squire you around in Singapore for three weeks."

"He's being well paid to—as you put it—squire me around," she flashed. "And that's why he can afford to take the time off. So where exactly does the predatory buzzard bit come in?"

Eric groaned mentally. He had not wanted things to be like this. He had come to see Anne off on her long flight east. He had not come to fight. He shook his head. "Let's just leave it—"

"No. That's not good enough, Eric. You started this with your snide remark. I don't know what you're trying to imply. I'm not naive enough to have failed to recognize that Jason pays court to me, flatters me, treats me like a woman, for God's sake! But for you to suggest—"

"I'm not really suggesting anything," Eric interrupted wearily. "I suppose it's basically a matter of surprise to me that Sullivan is concentrating on Morcomb Enterprises business when he could be picking up fat fees in the City, but all right, you're paying him well. Look, I'm sorry, it's the thought that I won't be seeing you for three weeks—"

"It's not as though we've been spending much time together during the last two years" she observed cuttingly.

It was true. His preoccupation with the Quayside practice, his dislike of the county circles they moved in, and her own expanding business interests had meant they seemed to have begun to lead separate lives. Perhaps it needed saying—but if there was a fault in their lifestyle, it lay at both doors. He looked at her. The grey eyes were angry, and unforgiving, and yet he felt they also contained a hint of guilt, as though she recognized she was being unreasonable, not recognizing the tension that lurked in him. But if there was guilt, she shrugged it off. "I don't have time for this," she said. "Or the inclination. I'm sorry you bothered coming to see me off at all."

He was sorry too. It would have been better had it been left as it was last night, with her warm in his arms, a soft moonlight in the room, and the feeling that they had not really drifted apart at all, in the years of their life together at Sedleigh Hall.

He watched the plane take off from his car in the car park. It was early afternoon and the sun had broken through after the light spattering of rain that had darkened the tarmac. He sat there for a while after the thunder of the plane had faded in the sharp February air and he thought about his own insecurities, how they had never before really affected the pattern of his life. He had the feeling they were about to do so now. He had to face the bitterness of his emotions: he had a wealthy, attractive wife who was younger than him, and he was jealous, possessive in a way he had never realized he was capable of, and he resented the fact that she would be spending three weeks with a man he disliked, distrusted. And, perhaps, envied.

The thoughts in his mind were unpleasant and he despised himself for them, and the corrosive images they thrust upon him.

He started the car and made his way back towards Newcastle, and his small office on the Quayside.

He could have expanded the business over the years but had chosen not to do so. A one-man practice suited him: he chose to deal only with those matters that interested him, and although the occasional fat shipping contract had come his way, in the main he concentrated on matters of small moment. It was a world that some would describe—had described—as low-life, the drunks, the drop-outs, the desperate and the inadequates that Tyneside spawned, but it was a world he knew. He had experienced it as a copper on the beat, and he was disinclined to move far from it even though if he had chosen to follow the contacts that Martin and Channing's mercantile bank brought him his practice could have been very different. The business suited him: he felt he was dealing with real people, with real and very personal problems. In which, sometimes, he could help.

It was *his* world, not a world into which he had been invited by Anne's friends and contacts.

He entered at the side door as usual and made his way up the stairs: it enabled him to enter his room unobserved by those who might be in the reception room. He might have a low-life practice, but that didn't mean he was prepared to deal with all the Tyneside detritus that washed up against his doors.

He flopped down into the chair behind his desk, still dispirited from his encounter with Anne, and buzzed the intercom. "I'm back, Susie. You need to see me?"

She entered a few minutes later.

Susie Cartwright was a forty-year-old widow who had been working for him for two years. She was practical, intensely loyal, occasionally critical and always outspoken. She kept her hair cut severely short, she gave the impression of cool disdain in her manner, but she was efficient and if her glance could sometimes be darkly disapproving he had the consolation of knowing he would soon learn what her moods were all about. He guessed that, like all secretaries, she knew more about him than he realized.

She pushed some papers in front of him. "These need your signature. I thought you were in court this afternoon."

"Got away early. Saw Anne off."

"I see. Everything all right?"

He glanced up at her. There was a certain curiosity in her eyes, but it was well-meaning. He nodded. "The plane was on time."

"Good." She seemed to be on the point of saying something else, but then thought better of it. As he scribbled his signature she stood beside his desk. When he'd finished, she gathered up the papers and headed for the door. "I'll be leaving in an hour or so. You remember you have that awards dinner to go to this evening? Oh, and Mr Leonard Channing rang to say he won't be able to make it, and to present his apologies."

Eric grimaced. "Apologies? To whom? He's not a guest of honour, or anything."

She shrugged. "To Mr Hallam, I imagine."

"Hallam? Yes, he'll be there, I suppose. But we're meeting him tomorrow, anyway. Channing will be at that meeting, I trust?"

"An early flight from London." She hesitated in the doorway. "You've no other clients booked in for this afternoon, because of the scheduled court hearing, but there is someone in reception who wants to see you."

"And?"

"I don't know whether *you* want to see *him.*"

Susie Cartwright had that in common with his wife, Eric thought. She enjoyed working with him, but she did not approve of the kind of clients he sometimes took on. He knew she was of the view he should move up-market. "What's his name?"

"Stevens. I don't think you know him. And if you want my view…" The words died on her lips as she caught the quizzical look on his face. She tightened her lips and flounced out of the room. A short while later she was back, opening the door. "Mr Stevens," she announced, and closed the door behind him as the man entered to take the seat offered by Eric.

Stevens was in his early thirties, Eric calculated. He was of the kind of build commonly associated with the mining fraternity: broad shoulders, deep chest, narrow waist and short in the leg. In a different generation he might have been hacking for coal in the Vane Tempest mines, but times had changed: Eric suspected this man would have been trained in the violence of the West End streets, built up his muscular torso in the local gyms, gained his experience of life around the nightclubs and drinking dens, and while the palms of his hands would be soft, the knuckles would be hard, with signs of old breaks. He was pale, broken-nosed, and dressed well enough in a cheap, brash way. His eyes were never still, as though always seeking the main chance that never seemed to come his way. There was an overall air of failure about him, worn like a faded flower pinned to his buttonhole. Eric had seen a thousand like him over the years, on the beat and in his office. He could understand why Susie objected to his presence in the office. He was not the kind of client she wished to see.

"Well, Mr Stevens, what can I do for you?"

The man wriggled in his seat, uncomfortable, his eyes darting around the room, fishing for support. "I'm looking for protection."

Eric smiled. "A curious word. Are you sure you're in the right place?"

“I been told you was straight.”

“That’s comforting. So...?”

Stevens hesitated. “I been in trouble, from time to time, but the word on the street is that don’t matter to you. You’ll help anyway.”

Eric frowned. Cautiously, he said, “I’ll help if I can, and if it’s legal help you want. It depends what you mean by protection.”

“I’m being set up, Mr Ward.”

“In what way?”

Stevens hesitated, a blurred indecision in his eyes. “Burglary. Breaking and entering.”

Eric observed the man in the chair opposite him. He thought for a little while, caught the slight shiver in the man’s hands and became more aware of the shifting desperation of the glances he threw about the corners of the room. He drew a legal pad in front of him, and picked up a pen. “All right, what are you on?”

“Eh?”

“Drugs.”

“I didn’t say…” Stevens wriggled uncertainly, then took a deep breath, uncertainty slithering into his voice. “I need a snort, that’s for sure. But that’s not my problem. It’s got nothing to do with it. I’m here because I’m being harassed, and the police have got it wrong, but with my record they’ll be out to nail me and—”

“Tell me about your record,” Eric said calmly.

Stevens was unwilling, but as Eric stared him down he shivered again, and complied. “I come out of the Meadow Well estate, Mr Ward. There’s not much choice out there, you know, except for villainy. So I ran with the gangs and I got into trouble. A bit of GBH here and there, lifted a few things, you know how it is.” He paused, and a certain cunning crept into his manner. “There’s this thing called lawyer’s privilege, isn’t that so?”

“It’s *client’s* privilege,” Eric explained. “I can’t disclose to third parties what you tell me in this office, as my client.”

“I thought that was the way of it,” Stevens remarked smugly. “Right, well like I said, I ran with a bad lot and I got into a bit of trouble—”

“Including burglary?”

"Didn't everyone?" Stevens almost jeered. "I mean, down there, we even lifted from each other! But that was years ago. I been making a living for myself away from that for a couple of years. Livin' by my wits, you might say."

"And what does that mean?"

Stevens shrugged pride into his stocky shoulders, a burden he rarely carried. "The race track. The casinos. I got a lucky streak, you see: I can play the tables, and I can pick the horses. I been doing well couple of years now. And burglary and that sort of stuff, it's way behind me."

"But now you've been set up," Eric reminded him patiently. "If the police have something on you from the past, it is natural that they'll come after you if there's a hint that you might have been involved."

"It ain't the polis—I mean, they are on my back, but it's not them who've set me up."

"You'd better explain," Eric suggested wearily.

Stevens hunched forward confidentially, smoothing at his wrinkled brow in a vague desperation. "It's like this. I told you, I been making a living at the Newcastle race track and I been doing well, there, and at the dogs. They don't like me too much, the bookies," he added, drawing about him rags of pride. "They don't like losin' money, you know? But I also been working the casinos, and the clubs. There've been a few games I managed to get in on…until I realized I was bein' ripped off. The hands were rigged."

"You mean you started losing?"

"Started? By God, they tore into me a couple of times, and then I had a bad run at the track, and that's when Mad Jack Tenby put the boot in."

"Tenby?" Eric raised his eyebrows. He knew about Mad Jack. His name was a byword on Tyneside: he was rumoured to have a hand in most of the organized criminal activities along the river, over the years. A tall brute of a man with a marked face from old fights twenty years ago, he had yet managed to distance himself somewhat from his background by moving into seemingly legitimate enterprises such as nightclubs in Newcastle, Shields and Sunderland. He dressed well these days, giving himself the appearance of a well-insured man but it was still rumoured that though he covered his tracks pretty well, his fingers were pulling the strings on a number of major activities along the Tyne—prostitution, gambling and extortion. Eric had seen him often enough in the old days, at police dinners: he had always managed to get an invitation. The word was it was one way of keeping tabs on him. To Eric's mind, there was another explanation—corruption.

"You upset big people," Eric suggested. He eyed Stevens with scepticism. "But why would Tenby put the boot in to you? How much money is involved?"

Stevens shuffled uncomfortably in his seat. "Not more than twenty grand. But that's not the point. And I don't mean it's Mad Jack personally who's taking me on. There's his enforcer—he's a mad bastard too, and it'll be him who's setting me up. You see, they could hammer me, break a few bits of me, and that'd be par for the course. But what they got in mind is a prison sentence, a remand, and that's a different matter. There's a few characters inside who'd welcome me with open arms. And that way Mad Jack wouldn't be involved, but the message would go out, wouldn't it?"

Eric leaned back in his chair, and folded his arms. "Are you seriously suggesting Tenby—or his enforcer—would frame you on a burglary charge to get you inside, where they could get you sorted—"

"It's the truth, Mr Ward," Stevens interrupted eagerly. "I never went near that house in Gilsland—it's way off my roads. But the police reckon they got a tip-off, and they got proof, and they intend throwing the book at me, and then I get this phone call from Terry Morton—"

Eric held up his hand. "Terry Morton. And who might he be?"

"Mad Jack's enforcer," Stevens explained hurriedly. "He wanted the money, like now, or else. But I know what he was driving at. It's the money, or I go inside...damn it, you know how things are with some of the coppers. Tenby pulls their strings, and they'd be more than happy to put low-life like me away, even if it meant me getting cut by old acquaintances inside."

Eric shook his head. Wearily, he asked, "So what do you want me to do?"

"Represent me. Gimme help. I can pay you—"

"When you owe twenty thousand?" Eric smiled.

"There's ways, Mr Ward."

"I'm sure there are. But I don't want to know." He hesitated, observing Stevens for a little while. The man was clearly anxious, fear flickering in his eyes, and the comment about the police had struck home with Eric. He knew well enough there were one or two men on the force who were tight with Tenby and his organization. He could even name the odd one. He grunted, making up his mind. "All right, I'll see what I can do."

"You'll take it on?" Stevens asked eagerly.

Eric nodded. "I'll make no promises, but I'll make some inquiries, see if I can find out whether you're telling the truth. Then...well, I'll see what I can do. Meanwhile, there are some formalities. Your surname's Stevens. For the record, what's your full name?"

"Henry. Just Henry. But most people know me as Tramline Stevens."

"Why?"

Eric Ward's new client hesitated for a moment, then drew back the sleeve of his jacket. His arm was muscular, but corded with thick, clogged veins. They writhed up his arm like sluggish white snakes.

"Obvious, innit?"

2

Eric showered and changed at the flat that he and Anne still retained in Gosforth. It was convenient, for there were often times when one or both of them needed to stay in the city, and it could be a long drive home to Sedleigh Hall in the late evenings after a long, tiring day or convivial occasion.

He was not looking forward to the awards reception that was being held at the Gosforth Park Hotel that evening. It was the kind of shindig he normally avoided: held basically for commercial purposes, with financial support from a local newspaper, it gave certain individuals an opportunity for transitory glory, receivers of applause from men and women who all thought they deserved the award more than the recipient on the stage. The people attending would consist of people afraid of not being seen, wanting to maintain spurious business contacts; they would be accompanied by bored spouses or partners, the small-talk would be banal, the acquaintances slender and those on the fringe of the activity would be obsequious, pressing business cards on unwilling recipients as the noise got louder in conjunction with the increase in alcoholic intake, and the conversation more inane.

He would have been inclined to skip the whole thing, particularly in his general mood of depression at the moment, but he had nothing better to do and he had accepted the invitation at the behest of Leonard Channing, chairman of city mercantile bankers Martin and Channing. "We need to be seen there, Eric, there are a few people you should meet..." Eric doubted that the occasion would be a rewarding one, and he was also somewhat annoyed now that he had heard Channing himself would not in fact be present.

Eric cursed the chairman of the merchant bank as he struggled with his bow tie. The old fox generally managed to find reasons to avoid situations that were either boring or troublesome. Eric was not sure into which category the business awards dinner would fall.

The Jaguar was parked in the garage under the apartment block where Eric and Anne had their flat. He had used the Toyota earlier when he had gone out to the airport, but decided on the change if only to raise a few eyebrows: some of the other lawyers there might think his business was picking up. He spent little time in their company outside the courtroom, so it was no bad idea to keep them guessing.

It was not a long drive to the Gosforth Park Hotel and it was a deliberate decision on his part to set out late: he wanted to spend the least time possible at the event, consonant with good manners. Though why he was bothering, he was not sure: the awards reception was notable for its long-winded speeches—platitudinous and laced with bad old jokes—and for the generous amount of free alcohol consumed.

The reception was in full swing when he arrived. There were perhaps eighty people in the room, and most were already advancing towards a barely civilized drunkenness. There was an almost equal number of men and women, a few trophy wives, the odd girlfriend, but the men tended to be middle-aged, inclining towards the portly, greying or bald. They wore their success like tarnished badges, their spouses brittle and knowing. He spoke to a few acquaintances; they asked after Anne and how Morcomb Enterprises were getting along, but they were not really interested in the replies, their eyes sliding glances elsewhere as he spoke. None mentioned his own practice. It was a widely held view in this kind of gathering that Eric Ward was a queer kind of fish: a man with a well-heeled wife, business interests in the City, and yet he continued to scrabble around in the lower echelons of Tyneside society. So he drifted, sipping a whisky, listening as little as possible to the speeches and making small conversation until he was surprised to see a face he knew well.

The man who had just entered the room was tall, bulging somewhat at the waist and looking rather uncomfortable in a dinner jacket. He was in his late fifties now, and his bulbous nose was red-veined, his sharp blue eyes half hidden by sad, fleshy lids. He exuded an assumed air of easy bonhomie, but Eric could remember days in the nick when Detective Sergeant—now Detective Chief Inspector—Sampson had laid the boot into more than a few suspects and persuaded them of his hardness. But the years had changed him: his heavy features sagged with the weight that limited professional success could bring. Eric moved towards him, touched him on the elbow.

"Not exactly your line, Sammy."

"Eric! How you been keeping, bonny lad? Still waging war for the criminal fraternity?"

Eric grinned. "You know me better than that. Would I wage war against the police, when I used to be one myself?"

Sampson showed yellowing teeth and grabbed a glass of whisky from a passing waiter. He waved it in Eric's direction.

"Some said when you left us, that you was a turncoat, becoming a lawyer."

"You one of those, Sammy?"

"Naw. I knew the reasons. How are things with the eyes, these days?"

"Under control, more or less," Eric replied carefully. "What are you doing here at this reception, anyway?"

Sampson winked broadly, and grinned, but the edges of his mouth were stiff. "Keepin' an eye on the other half, you know. Naw, that's not really it, I picked up a job with the hotel...head of security."

"You're finishing with the force?"

"Already have. Last weekend." Sampson sucked at his teeth, and gave Eric a sideways glance. There was the dry-leaved rustle of regret in his voice. "You know how it is—every so often the top brass want a change, bring in new blood. And there's always favours to be called in. So, when the Chief suggested I might like to leave it was sort of arranged that a certain job be made available to me." He shrugged. "Too good an offer to turn down."

"So they wanted to push someone up into your job?"

"Not exactly." Sampson sipped at his drink, his mouth souring somewhat. "Anyway, I'm here on sort of duty, even if I do have to wear a dinner jacket. You, you're here to enjoy yourself. The wife here?"

Sampson knew Anne. Eric was aware that he was one of those among the police on Tyneside who had at one time envied him his good fortune, marrying a wealthy young woman. Somewhat uncomfortably, reminded of the tension of that afternoon, Eric said, "No, Anne's in South-East Asia, on business."

"That so? Pity. Bonny lass. I liked her. Haven't seen her in a while."

To change the subject, Eric asked, "So if you've finished, who's replacing you on the crime squad?"

Sampson barked a short laugh. He shook his head, resentment shimmering in his eyes. "You wouldn't know him. A chap called Charlie Spate. There are those along the docks thought I was a right bastard, but I tell you, Spate's something else again. Come in on a transfer from the Met. Got his own ideas. Hard as nails, and nasty with it. Even with his mates, you know what I mean?"

"Did he transfer for promotion?"

"Seems not. The gossip suggests maybe it was time for him to leave the Met, you know? But no one can say why...whether it was he got too close to villains, or whether he got too uncomfortable to live with on the force. Aye, it's going to be interestin' to see how Charlie Spate settles down to life in the North."

"Villains are villains wherever they operate, Sammy."

"You're right there, bonny lad."

They both stood there, grinning, and almost by mutual consent began rocking slightly on their heels like caricature policemen, looking around at the noisy gathering, feeling part of it and yet excluded, different, never exactly friends, yet bound together by a common background. After a short while, Eric asked, "You ever come across Mad Jack Tenby?"

"More than enough. Smooth bastard these days, but he used to be a crazy one when he was young." He eyed Eric suspiciously, his gaze tangled with conflicting reminiscences. "Don't tell me you're low enough to be acting for him these days!"

Eric laughed. "Hardly. But I've got a client who reckons Tenby's set him up on a burglary charge."

"Why would the old bugger do that?"

Eric shrugged. "My client suggests he's been framed because of debts he owes Tenby."

"Gambler, hey?" Sampson considered the matter, scratching his chin. "Could be true, of course. Tenby's changed. Time was he'd have strong-armed a debt himself, broken a leg or two—and a few fly characters have disappeared into the Tyne in the old days. But Mad Jack tries to look more legit these days: his nightclubs are supposed to be straight, though my own bet is they're financed by some funny money. Still, he's cleaned up his act, is invited to high-class dos, started moving among the hoi polloi, if you know what I mean. So, a set-up like the one you suggest could be a cleaner way for him...putting someone inside, instead of thumping the hell out of him. I've no doubt Tenby's got enough connections inside the walls to make life just as uncomfortable for your client, and even more so, than outside. And Tenby's clean of it." He hesitated. "You want to tell me who your client is?"

"Not really." Eric hesitated. "The charge concerns a robbery at Gilsland."

Sampson was silent for a while. "Colonel Lansbury's place," he said after a while. "It was one of my files—Charlie Spate's got hold of it now. So it's Tramline Stevens you're acting for, is it? I tell you, Eric, you always did stick your neck out for the wrong people. That little bastard deserves all he gets—whether it's from us, or from Mad Jack Tenby. He's a right little villain."

"That's not really the point, Sammy. The question is, did he do the burglary at Gilsland? Or is he being set up?"

"Well, I'll tell you this for nothing. What I had on the file, tip-off, forensics and all that, it was enough to convince me we could put him inside. I don't think you got much goin' for you on this one, bonny lad—"

He broke off as there was the crash of broken glass and voices raised, followed by a slap that sounded like a gunshot in the suddenly quietening room. With Sampson, Eric looked back behind him. Some twenty feet away across the room a small group was breaking up: one of them, a red-faced, middle-aged, self-important man in an expensive dinner jacket was arguing angrily with two men who held him by the arm. He was struggling, glaring over his shoulder at a tall blonde woman in an off-the-shoulder black evening dress. She had classical, fine-boned features and she held her head high as she glared at the angry man. It was clear she had just slapped him, and his friends were trying to pull him away. As they did so, two younger men spoke quietly to the girl and she nodded, allowed herself to be led away towards the bar. She moved easily, confidently, but with a certain disdainful arrogance, contemptuous of the scene that had been caused and of the stares she collected from the older women, and the trophy wives, and the girls who were there because they had been invited.

The man who had been slapped was still struggling, and he

clearly did not think this was the end of the affair. He was trying to break free of the hands that restrained him, and was all for following the young woman to the bar.

"There it goes," Sampson said resignedly. "No peace for the wicked. Like I said, I'm on duty, so...we have here a belligerent guest maybe taking a bit too much to drink, so it's time I started using my experience, and my noted powers of persuasion, not to mention my bulk, to cool things down."

Eric watched with a certain amusement as ex-Detective Chief Inspector Sampson walked in measured stride towards the still expostulating man and took his elbow. He gave him a beaming smile, whispered something in his ear. For a moment the man seemed angry, then Sampson said something else to him, at the same time easing him away from the others, and when the two men finally made their way towards the fringe of the party they seemed to be on almost amicable terms.

"An impressive show," someone said behind Eric. "An ex-colleague of yours from way back, I believe?"

Eric turned. It was Joe Hallam. "We were both policemen, yes. You're well informed, Mr Hallam."

Hallam smiled, his white teeth gleaming against his tanned skin. "I make it a point, always get to know who's who. That's why, when Leonard Channing told me you'd be handling the Barker Marine purchase for me, I took the trouble to ask around about you. Interesting."

Coolly, Eric replied, "I'm glad you found it so."

"Interesting...and unusual. Ex-copper, solicitor, and married into money." When Eric made no reply, Hallam went on, "I hear the hotel taking Sampson on was a favour to the Chief Constable. Good appointment. That situation was handled well, and discreetly."

Eric observed the man speaking to him. He did not know a great deal about Joe Hallam's background. He was not a local man, but had come to the north-east some ten years ago, and had got busy in the construction industry. He had made money quickly, and soon moved among the moneyed entrepreneurs who made their living along the Tyne and Wear. He was known to keep himself largely to himself. no great extravagances, no wild living. He was also single: though being tall, good-looking in a rugged sort of way, with dark hair frosted at the temples and a wide, Latin mouth, he had no trouble finding women who were attracted to him. But they tended to be of a kind because for all his surface finesse Joe Hallam had an innate coarseness of attitude and turn of phrase on occasions. He was reputed to be a bully, and rode roughshod over the competition. Now he turned cold dark eyes on Eric and asked, "So you've got everything in hand for tomorrow's meeting?"

"I think so."

"Channing not here?"

"He'll be arriving in the morning."

Hallam's mouth twisted dismissively. "Can't be bothered this evening, hey? I was expecting him here. Arrangements had been made..." He paused, a certain wariness seeping into his cold, appraising eyes. "Anyway, no matter...I've already briefed him—I want the Barkers screwed down tomorrow. This whole business has gone on too long: they've been delaying me, buggering up the whole project all winter. I'd hoped and expected that we'd be starting construction within a month, but now Leonard tells me..." His glance flickered away around the room, dwelling for a moment on the tall blonde woman who had been the centre of the earlier quarrel. He stared at her for a few moments, and then abruptly his glance slid back to Eric. "Fact is, I want you to thrust the knife in tomorrow. Leonard has the details. You'd better mug up on them early, before the meeting. I don't want any more delays." He looked again towards Sampson, now amiably chatting to the mollified businessman, and then back to the laughing blonde at the bar. "Silly bitch...making an exhibition of herself," he muttered. Then he turned, moving away, nodded to Eric. "See you at the cavalry charge."

As he walked away he donned a mask of affability, slapping backs, using names, making jokes, calling for individual glasses to be filled, moving confidently through the crowd. Eric watched his progress: he did not like him, and he had a bad feeling about the Barker Marine business. Leonard Channing never got Eric Ward involved in a consultancy matter for the merchant bank unless he felt there were problems in it that might trip up the younger man. Channing had always resented Eric on the board, and had made it a challenge to try to get rid of him. He hadn't succeeded. Yet.

Eric stayed longer at the reception than he had intended. He was careful to drink very little, but he had a further discussion with Sampson after the mollified businessman had left. Once they got talking about old times when they had been on the force together, villains they had known, pubs they had closed on the beat, and investigations Sampson had conducted, the time had slipped away and Eric realized that most of the people had left the party, drifting off to other destinations. He looked at his watch. It was eleven o'clock. Time to go home. Sampson was disinclined to follow him.

"I got nowhere to go, and the booze is free here. Good to see you, Eric. Keep in touch."

The car park was half empty. Rear car lights flashed as a car drove out and then there was the sound of someone trying to start an engine, the sluggish, complaining motor echoing in the cavernous dimness of the underground car park. Eric headed for the Jaguar, pressed his electronic key and there was an orange flashing of lights. He opened the door, got in and settled himself, putting the ignition key in the lock. The engine rumbled into life immediately, and he swung the car out into the centre lane to leave the car park.

Pinned in his headlights was a woman, one hand shielding her eyes, the other held in front of her as though warding him off. Her features were blank, washed out, almost indiscernible in the reflection of the headlights, and she carried a dark jacket over her arm, but he recognized the low-cut black dress. He slowed, stopped, and she walked towards the driver's side.

"You know anything about bloody cars?" she asked.

Her voice was low and throaty; she was also rather drunk. He was very much aware of her cleavage as she leaned towards him, one hand on the roof of the car. She had a bosom that could be described only as magnificent.

"What's the trouble?"

"Damn thing won't start. You any good at that sort of thing?"

"I'm afraid not," he admitted. "I could lift the bonnet, and I could recognize the engine but that's about it. I'm afraid my talents, such as they are, aren't mechanical."

"Sod it!" She looked almost wildly around her. "I can't stay here. And half the cars are gone." She swung back to him. "You'll have to give me a lift home."

There was a surprisingly fierce edge to her tone, a panicked tremor in her voice as though she was anxious, worried about something other than the breakdown of her car. Eric supposed she did have something to worry about: a beautiful young woman alone in a car park, even in Gosforth, would hardly feel other than vulnerable. He hesitated. "Where do you live?"

"Across town. Fenham. I'll show you." She was already making her way around to the passenger seat. There was little he could do, other than agree to take her home.

They left the car park and headed towards Newcastle. Her address was not a great deal out of his way, but he was glad now that he had remained fairly abstemious as far as the alcohol was concerned. She huddled in the seat beside him, her arms crossed over her chest, her eyes fixed on the road ahead. After a while, she glanced at him, watched him for a little while. He found it disconcerting. Suddenly, she said, "I saw you at the reception."

"Is that right? I saw you too."

"Who didn't?" she muttered sourly. Then her attitude changed. She giggled suddenly, as though recalling the incident in which she'd been involved, but it was overlaid by a nervous tension. She turned her head, to look back to the dark road behind her. Then she fixed her attention on him again. "Someone...someone said you were a lawyer."

"Of sorts..."

She fell silent. He drove on for some twenty minutes. He peered forward at the road signs. "Your address...is it somewhere around here?"

"Half a mile on, then first left. Right at the roundabout, and you'll see a block of serviced flats. That's where I live."

He followed her directions. He found the flats easily enough but discovered that he was faced with a one-way street sign that prevented him drawing near to the building itself. There were some spaces among the parked cars in the street: she pointed to one. "You can pull in there."

It was some fifty yards from the main entrance to the apartment building. The area was not well lit. Eric hesitated. "Would you like me to see you to your door?"

"No." She got out of the car, swinging long legs in a graceful motion. She turned, looked down at him. "No. I want you to come up."

He hesitated, uncertain.

"I've got a problem," she asserted.

"I'm not sure—"

"I've got a problem," she snapped, "and you're a bloody lawyer, aren't you?"

3

He was sure he was making a mistake.

On the other hand what else could he do? She was blonde, beautiful and she was in distress: he had detected a clear anxiety in her manner from the moment she had approached him in the car park. So he felt he had little choice other than, at least, to escort her to the door of her apartment. But no further. He would politely, but firmly suggest that if she really did have a problem she should make an appointment to see him at his office next day.

Somehow, things did not work out that way.

The apartment block was rather more elegant than he had expected: the security system at the front door hall was old hat, but the lift was silent and efficient, well-carpeted, the corridor on the fourth floor had been recently painted, albeit dimly lit, and when she swung open the door to her apartment he could see it was tastefully and expensively furnished.

She strode into the room and flung aside the light jacket she had been wearing. "God, I need a drink!"

He hesitated in the doorway. "Look, I think I'd better—"

"Come in and close the door. I need some advice as well as a drink! What's your particular poison?"

"Er...if you've got some brandy, and water..." He entered, closed the door behind him, still uncertain, but reasoning that it might be better if he took a drink with her, found out what the problem was: it would be the best way to handle things. She was already half drunk, he suspected, so maybe it was just as well that she hadn't been able to start her car.

"So, brandy and water," she said, and placed the glass on a low table in front of the settee. "Sit down," she ordered, left the room and came back with a glass of whisky for herself. She flopped down on the other end of the settee, picked up her glass and raised her eyes to his. They were knowing in their intensity.

"Cheers."

He sipped his drink, aware of her open scrutiny.

"So what's your name?"

"Eric Ward. And yours?"

"Sandra Vitali."

She was about five feet eight, he guessed, and her eyes were an indeterminate green, somewhat shadowed by a vague uncertainty. He doubted whether the colour of her hair was natural but it was long and fashionably cut. Her features were regular and classical, except for the slight tip-tilting of her nose. She lay sprawled carelessly on the settee, the low cut black dress revealing the first swell of her bosom, and her long legs stretched out, her knee almost touching his. She exuded a nervous sexuality; sensuality shadowed by anxiety. He sipped his drink: the glass contained more brandy than soda.

"So you said you had a problem."

She nodded. She seemed more relaxed now, with a drink in her hand, in her own apartment. "You married?"

He hesitated, then nodded.

"Most men I've known are," she said in a matter-of-fact tone. There was a glint of appraisal in her green eyes. "You're not bad looking."

It was not the sort of conversation he was comfortable with. To deflect her, he said, "The man you had the altercation with at the reception...is *he* married?"

Anger flared into her tone. "That pig! He had the nerve to proposition me right in front of everyone. All right, I went with him once, but that gave him no right to treat me like I was a whore!" Her nervousness fading, she giggled, unexpectedly, at the thought. "Though I've never been any better than I should have been, I have to admit."

"Is that the problem you want to discuss with me?" Eric asked, trying to get her back on course. "The man at the reception—"

The attempt was unavailing. She took a stiff pull at her whisky and waved the glass at him in an extravagant gesture, as though outlining the plains of her lost past. "You see, it wasn't easy for me. It's the classical story, of course: a mother who thought more of the gin bottle than her daughter; child abuse, a stepfather who pulled off my knickers when I was barely twelve, then jealous quarrels with my mother when he started bringing me presents. After that, by the time I was fourteen I wanted out, then kicking against the traces, getting in with the wrong group, you've heard it all before, I expect, being a lawyer."

"It's a familiar enough story, certainly."

"But the lights were so bright in London, and life was exciting and I found I could make a decent living there...with the right men. But, well, I came back north in tow with an attractive man—how old do you reckon I am?"

"I never guess at women's ages...not openly, at least."

"I'm twenty-seven," she smirked, "but I seen a lot more than twenty-seven years' living."

"I don't doubt it. But you said you wanted help with a problem."

She struggled to a more upright position, and shifted nearer to him on the settee. "I need a knight in shining armour," she muttered, "to get out of the mess I'm in. You never know how deep the water's going to be when you splash right in, do you? And I'm in way over my head."

She eyed him, one eyebrow raised reflectively. "That old lecher bugged me tonight; I lost control. I had too much on my mind. Then I saw you, asked about you. When I heard you were a lawyer I thought maybe I'd contact you. But then, by lucky chance, it was you who picked me up in the car park...Bloody car..."

"What sort of mess is it?"

"The worst," she said, eyeing him speculatively. There was a short silence. "How come you haven't made a pass at me yet?"

Eric ignored the question. "You asked me here because you have a problem."

"And because you're an attractive man. A combination that appeals to me. Funny thing is, I was scared back at the car park, and still worried even when we were driving here. But now you're here in my apartment, I feel safe..."

"It could be the alcohol," he said dryly.

"No, it's you. I've been tense, scared...But I feel safe with you here...and curious."

She fixed him with a speculative gaze; then, before he realized what she was doing she slid along the settee, put one hand on his shoulder and kissed him. Her lips were soft, the kiss exploratory, her tongue flickering against his mouth. He made no attempt to draw away, but resisted the impulse to respond. "Gentle," she murmured appreciatively.

"Miss Vitali—"

"Sandra. You said you were married." She was leaning across him, her breasts half exposed. He could see the tic of the vein in her throat, close to his shoulder. "So how come your wife wasn't with you this evening?"

"She's gone to Singapore for a few weeks."

"I see." Her glance lingered on him meaningfully, and she smiled; there was something in her green eyes that quickened his pulse. He was disturbed, unbalanced. She drained her glass. "Another?"

He hesitated, but to cover his confusion finished his drink and nodded, knowing even then he was getting even deeper into potential trouble. She was back in a little while with their replenished glasses. She sat beside him on the settee, her bare shoulder leaning against his.

"I think we'd better get something clear..." he began.

"Stop behaving like a coy virgin," she cut in. "Drink up, and maybe we can forget all our troubles…me with the mess I'm in, and you with your wife shoving off for a few weeks…by *herself,* I take it?"

Eric made no reply. Anne would not, of course, be by herself. That was the problem as far as he was concerned. He remembered the tension that had lain between himself and Anne at the airport, and a slow resentment seeped through his veins. He should have had the moral courage to tell her what he felt then, about the fact that Jason Sullivan was paying court to her and she seemed to be enjoying it, flirting with danger. He was convinced Sullivan was out to make a conquest, irrespective of the brief he held for Morcomb Enterprises, and Anne should have seen that, and should have realized how much it bothered her husband.

"Ah. So *not* alone, then," Sandra Vitali said, watching him through lidded eyes. "Well, there are all sorts of games that two can play."

When she kissed him again he could taste the whisky on her tongue, and this time he did not resist. Her body was pressing against his and her arm was around his neck. There was a deep sensuality about her mouth that stirred him, and the resentment that had begun to flood through him was changing gradually into desire. He responded to her, exploring her mouth. She leaned back and looked at him with contemplative eyes, languid with desire, then took his hand and slipped it into the top of her dress. Her breast was firm, its tip hard under his fingers, the skin cool and soft.

"This is not the way lawyer–client relationships should begin," he suggested huskily.

"Then let's leave the lawyer–client thing for a little while and develop a different kind of relationship…"

The sheets in the darkened bedroom were cool to the touch but his body seemed to be on fire. The ache in his loins was intense and her fingers sought him out, slim, knowing, and her lips slid over him, teasingly, professionally, until he twisted and turned and pressed deeply into her with a long, shuddering groan. Her tongue flickered against his like a serpent, probing; her hands encouraged his strength, and her body was long, and pliant, and slim with the wisdom of experience. Time slipped past as they moved and writhed together in an abandoned rhythm, wet and sliding in the darkness and she did things to him that were unknown, and brought him to the edge of explosion. But she held him off, eased him, brought him back again until she was ready herself, till she cried out to him and he knew he was not the master, as everything turned red and black behind his eyelids and the almost agonized shuddering they both experienced plunged them over into an abyss where the darkness was like a form of death.

It was only then, when his tautened muscles had slackened, when he lay spent on top of this stranger in the darkness that he realized what he was doing, thought of who he was, where he came from, and he felt himself contract, sliding from her wetness. She moaned slightly, clenched her thighs as though to hold him inside her, but he slipped away, rolled over, to lie beside her, the sweat cooling on his body, his mind raging at himself.

This had not been intended.

"That was good," she said to him in a cool, seductive whisper, replete, close to his ear.

"When you're in trouble, there's nothing like a good—"

He twisted sideways, sat up in the bed. "Sandra, this wasn't very sensible." His words sounded foolish, priggish, almost childishly puritanical even to himself. "You tell me you're in trouble, and I guess that's why we've ended up like this—but it's fuelled by anxiety, and tension, and it's meaningless. We hardly know each other, and if I'm to help you, this is not the way to do it."

She ran slim fingers down his backbone. "You could persuade me otherwise." He felt himself stir again.

"You've already helped me," she said, her tone almost purring. "Maybe I've been overreacting, frightened by ghosts that don't exist. I told you, I was scared back at that hotel car park. And you were there. Now, it doesn't seem as bad. Maybe I can see a way out of things by myself. But I'll still need your help."

"What's it all about?" he asked, turning his head to look at her. He could make out her features only dimly in the darkness, her long, damp blonde hair fanned out carelessly on the pillow.

She hesitated, her hand still caressing his back. "I want out of something. Out of the life I've been leading. And there's people who don't like that. I...we...I've made a try at it, but I'm not sure...At first I thought I could handle it, but I felt exposed tonight, vulnerable and so I wasn't so sure. I got scared."

"What is it exactly you want to escape from?"

She sighed. "What I am, I guess. What I've been. *Who* I am. Hell, it's a long story, even for a whore."

There was a short silence, as she seemed lost in thought, trawling over her past. "Were you with anyone at the reception?" Eric asked curiously.

She shook her head. "No. I was there by invitation, just in case."

"In case of what?"

"I told you. I'm a whore, or as near as dammit to one. But I thought things had changed...I know they changed, and I was getting out, but now I'm not so sure. They told me—"

"Who's they.?"

She was silent for a little while. Then she reached for him again. "I don't want to talk about it right now. Let's do it again. I can forget about things for a while if we do it again. Then, in the morning, we can talk..."

"I don't think that's a good idea." Eric stood up, moved away from the bed. "Sandra, if you're in trouble, let's talk about it by all means. But this...this was a mistake. I can't think straight with you like this. I'm leaving now. Come to see me—"

"You could see me here."

"No," he replied firmly. "At the office. Come to see me there. And we can talk. This way, it's no good. I'm going to have to go."

"God, you *are* married!" she snapped suddenly, and rolled over away from him, her whole personality seeming to retreat from him like a cat from a dog, hissing and spitting.

He dressed in a confusion of emotions. He still desired her, and he could still remember the touch of her mouth, her hands, the tautness of her thighs as they wrapped themselves about his body, but there were other thoughts too—the surging post-coital guilt, recognition of acts of betrayal, his anger at what might happen in Singapore, the resentment at himself for having reacted in such a male, egotistical way, sating himself physically to avoid thinking about his own anxieties.

"Give me a ring later this morning," he said.

She lay on the rumpled sheets, her head turned away in scorn. She made no response.

Quietly, he let himself out of the apartment and waited for the lift down to the hallway. He thought he heard a slight noise down the corridor, towards the emergency stairs but when he turned his head he saw nothing. The lift arrived, he entered, and moments later he was at the ground floor. The front door was already open: he grunted, realizing the security system was far from operable. He walked slowly back to his car, but halfway there he stopped, leaned against the fencing that abutted on a small park area and looked up at the sky.

The February evening was sharp and cold and the sky studded with stars. Anne was still somewhere up there, would soon be arriving at her destination. She was probably asleep, oblivious, high above the earth. He took a deep breath. What the hell was he up to, allowing himself to be seduced by a practised woman such as Sandra Vitali? He wondered if it was her real name. Then he recalled the softness of her body, her firm breasts under him, the surging climactic wetness of her and he grunted in annoyance at himself. If she was already in a mess, so he was on the verge of getting himself into one.

He stood there for several minutes trying to bring order to the chaos of his mind, control the renewed urgency of his body. Then he slowly walked to the car. He felt in his jacket pocket for the car keys. He was unable to find them.

His blood seemed to go cold. He cursed. He couldn't remember putting them down anywhere in Sandra Vitali's flat. But in the urgent, sexual scramble of their disrobing the keys could have fallen from his pocket. He looked about him—maybe he could walk home to Gosforth, get the keys later, tomorrow maybe, if she came to see him at the office. A stupid thought.

He'd have to go back to the flat for the keys. He didn't want to, but there was nothing else for it.

Angry with himself he retraced his steps reluctantly, shivering slightly in the cold night air. As he turned into the short pathway to the entrance of the apartment block he realized there were other people about: the front door was still open, and a man's figure was framed in the doorway, emerging from the block of flats. Under the light of the porch he caught a brief glimpse of the man's face as he brushed past, and then Eric, none too keen at being seen himself, averted his eyes and entered the hallway. He wondered vaguely whether the other man hurrying off into the darkness had experienced the kind of sensations he had enjoyed only a short while earlier.

Eric pressed for the lift. A few seconds later the doors whirred open and he entered, pressed for Sandra's floor. He walked down the dimly lit corridor until he came to the door he had left less than ten minutes earlier. He hesitated: the door was unlocked, partly open.

"Sandra?"

His voice echoed eerily in the corridor. There was no reply. Tentatively he put his hand on the door to push it further ajar: there was no resistance. The door slowly swung fully open. He stepped inside.

She was the first thing he saw. She was still naked, lying on the thick carpet a few feet into the room. A chair had been overturned, a vase of flowers in pieces on the floor where she had flailed unavailingly in her panic and terror. In the lifeless crumpling of her body, he barely recognized her: the tongue was black and swollen, the green eyes wide, staring, blank with the incomprehension of death; her head was twisted at an unnatural angle.

He dropped to one knee beside her and felt for a pulse but it was an automatic, useless gesture on his part.

Sandra Vitali's neck had been broken. The woman with whom he had slept less than half an hour ago was dead.

Chapter two

1

The mid-morning sun struggled weakly through the window of the office overlooking the boatyard. Beyond, the Tyne ran sluggishly, dark and turgid, towards the bend beyond which could be seen the towering cranes of the docks. The boardroom of Barker Marine Ltd was sparsely enough furnished: a well-used long table, scarred by ancient cigarette butts; wooden-armed chairs whose upholstery was worn and faded; it was clear that the members of the board had forsworn comfort, elegance and image in favour of the working environment from which they had come—the river shore—and concentrated on the business rather than its trappings.

And maybe that was the problem, Eric thought to himself.

"We now have the detailed information," he said, "and the position outlined by the accountants would seem to suggest that it could be argued that Barker Marine is almost a negative-worth company, in realistic terms. You have work in hand, but accumulated debts of almost two million; you have contracts in the offing, but it is unlikely that you can complete the work within the scheduled time; your equipment is in need of overhaul and replacement—"

"And the offer made by Mr Hallam is to be described almost as philanthropical."

The sarcasm in the interruption was unveiled. Eric raised his head to observe Fred Barker. The man was well-known on Tyneside: he was perhaps five ten in height but stooping now in his seventieth year. He still had a good head of silver-grey hair, which tended to emphasize the tanned, burned skin of a man who had spent his life in the sea winds of the North. He had sported mutton-chop whiskers since he was a young man, according to old photographs, and they were still much in evidence, and oddly reddish in colour. He was a local character, a man of rough tongue when the occasion demanded, tough, belligerent and straight. The fact that he was now almost crippled with arthritis had not affected his temper. And his dislike for Hallam was clear.

Joe Hallam sneered, and shook his head. "To describe me as philanthropically inclined is almost an insult," he declared. "Mr Barker, you and I both know I'm a hard-headed businessman, and I don't throw money at any project unless I feel I can make a buck or two out of it. The fact is, as Ward here has outlined, Barker Marine is on its beam ends and the offer I'm making for it—lock, stock and barrel—is a fair one. You can huff and puff and shout the odds as long as you like but it's time we stopped fat-arsing around. You're broke, and you know it. We know it. Yet you still keep chasing around the North trying to find finance when every last damn fool knows no one's going to put money into a collapsing business."

"Except you," the old man replied bitterly.

"No." Hallam's eyes were sharp and cold. "I'm not putting money into any deadbeat business. I'm just interested in acquiring your assets, selling them off and then redeveloping the whole site. I've got plans of my own and they don't involve propping up a business that's finished. I'll rejuvenate this whole area but with a viable business of my own. And you can die in peace knowing the future of your family is secure, financially, even though you made a pig's ear of the business this last twenty years."

Rick Barker leaned forward, putting one hand on his father's arm as the old man seemed ready to explode into a verbal confrontation with Hallam. "Now that's not quite how we see things, Mr Hallam."

He was more quietly spoken than the old man, nor did he even look like him. Taller, slimmer, more fair-skinned, he had gone prematurely bald at forty but his eyes were young, and though his manner was milder, he was reputed to have inherited his father's stubbornness. He had been educated in Sunderland to his father's evident and often-expressed pride, but his degree in marine engineering had not served to save the firm when recession hit the northern shipyards. As a small, independent family company Barker Marine had always lived off the subcontracted work that was obtained from the bigger operations, but over the years the contracts had gradually dried up as life on the Tyne had changed. The days of the old coal heaving were a century past; the war years that had seen fortunes for men building warships were a distant memory; and as the new technological age had dawned, and quickened, and building contracts had gone overseas to Japan and Korea and Germany so the capital base of Barker Marine had been eroded, the family holdings had been stripped in desperate attempts to keep the business going, and a long, gradual slide had resulted in the company no longer being able to pay its way.

"The fact is," Rick Barker explained, "we don't dispute the validity of your figures. And of course, we're very interested in the offer you've made for the company. We've made no secret of that though naturally we've sought other alternatives these last few months. But there are still certain matters we are unhappy about. There are certain guarantees that we would like to have built into the contract that you seem to have ignored—"

"I don't think you're in any position to ask for any guarantees at all," Hallam snapped. "For God's sake, this business is down the Swanee! Your workforce is ancient; your capital is expended; your machinery is out of date; you don't have an investor in sight who'd be prepared to refinance you! This business is dead, dammit, and any fool can see that. Now look here. This is what we're offering, but it's a one-off deal, let's be clear on that. Dump this deal, and we won't be coming back..."

Eric was only half listening as Hallam went over the details once again. He was watching Leonard Channing. The chairman of the merchant bank that was helping finance the Hallam takeover of Barker Marine had a self-satisfied, almost smug look on his lean, hawkish features. He had arrived at Newcastle Airport that morning, on the early morning flight. Eric had picked him up, as a matter of courtesy, and driven him to the meeting. Channing was in his late sixties now—patrician of features, narrow nose, thin lips, and eyes dark with the confidence that came from handling other people's money. His manner was always polished and he had the swift elegance of a snake. On the drive from the airport he had questioned Eric about the progress of the takeover documentation, and Eric had briefed him somewhat abstractedly, but he gained the impression that Channing barely seemed to be listening. It was as though he was hugging to himself some secret, serpentine pleasure, something he was unprepared to divulge to his companion, and Eric wondered what it was.

Channing still had that smirking look about his mouth now, slim, supple fingers steepled at his chin as Hallam finished his peroration.

Fred Barker was shaking his head angrily. His voice held none of the doubts that an old, crippled body could bring. "It won't do, Hallam. You don't seem to realize that what we have here at Barker's is an institution. It was my grandfather who started the business—"

"Oh, God save us," Hallam intoned in mock desperation.

"—and we built up a reputation over three generations. All right, we've struck rocks and we're holed badly, but that don't mean we just give up and sink without a fight. We've the crew to think about—men who've been with us almost all their working lives, men who trust us, men who've invested time and money and hard work—"

"That sort of guff cuts no ice with me, Barker," Hallam snapped.

Rick Barker leaned forward, reasonably. "All we're suggesting is that we build in some guarantees for the workforce. We feel we have an obligation towards them: they're friends as much as employees. We cannot simply walk away with the money you'll pay us and leave them in the lurch."

Hallam glared at him, then turned to look at his legal adviser. "*You* tell them," he grunted. "They don't seem able to understand what I'm saying."

Eric frowned, shook his head as though to clear it of the images that still crowded there. "The point Mr Hallam is trying to make is that the purchase price for Barker Marine is for its assets and land, including the river frontage and all licences it holds in relation to that frontage. But Mr Hallam has no intention of reviving the business itself. He has no interest in the business. His company—Shoreline Investments Ltd—will be looking at an entirely new venture to replace Barker Marine."

"*Your* business is dead and gone," snarled Hallam.

"The location, the area, the opportunities Mr Hallam is looking at would suggest that the current activity of the yards is no longer of interest. The intention is to redevelop the whole site: the business plans he has submitted for financing demonstrate a growing opportunity for leisure craft operating here. That means building new facilities, extending a marina site, dredging at the river bank to allow boats of deeper draught to enter the river at this point. This work will take perhaps two years. The workforce you currently have is not suitable for this kind of development. So Mr Hallam cannot give any guarantees about retention of the workforce because he cannot use the people who are presently working for you—"

"They'll be on the street, Barker, and that's the end of it," Hallam glowered. "Now can we cut out all this crap, and get down to the business of agreeing the figures—"

"Wait a minute," Fred Barker cut in, his anger only just under control. "You're forgetting one thing."

Hallam sighed theatrically. "And what would that be, old man?"

Barker's blue eyes blazed. "The Ministry of Defence contract. That's due to run from June first, and there's no way you could complete that without the current workforce. All we're asking is that you give us some guarantees, for God's sake, to protect the livelihoods of the men who've worked loyally for Barker Marine for thirty years and more in some cases. At the very least you could guarantee them work for the life of the Ministry contract—"

Hallam shook his head. "We're not even sure we'd want to

honour that contract in the long run. It's of no great importance to us. Sure, we've taken it into account when negotiating our price for the business but that doesn't mean we'll necessarily go along with the deal. The margins are tight and—"

"You're not telling me you'd settle for a price that includes a profit margin from the defence contract," Rick Barker said, raising his eyebrows, "and then possibly scuttle the contract anyway!"

Hallam shrugged. "We'd have to look at our margins, certainly, if it meant keeping your people on under guarantee we'd be reconsidering the whole thing again—"

"Which is where, perhaps, I should come in," Leonard Channing interrupted smoothly.

They all turned to look at him, Fred Barker with outright hostility—he distrusted men like Channing as a matter of course—and waited. Channing let the silence run for a little while as he pretended to consult some papers in front of him. Eric recalled the self- satisfied smirk, and wondered what was coming.

"As you'll be aware, gentlemen," Channing intoned, "the merchant bank of Martin and Channing has been arranging some of the short-term financing of this purchase, and has been acting as legal and financial advisers to the project. Mr Ward, here, has provided the legal input to Mr Hallam—in my case, I keep an eye on the commercial and financial implications of the project. The whole contractual aspect of the affair has been somewhat drawn out, mainly because of problems raised by you, Mr Barker—" He nodded towards the bewhiskered old man. Fred Barker leaned back in his chair and glowered.

"As far as Mr Hallam is concerned," Channing continued, "I now have to say that this delay has...ah...been somewhat to his advantage."

There was a short silence. Puzzled, Hallam turned his head slowly, to stare at Channing, who smiled thinly, nodding assurance. "Advantage?" Hallam growled. "This bickering has delayed us by three months!"

"As I say, advantage. It has prevented Shoreline Investments Ltd from stepping in to buy, as one might say, a pig in a poke."

Fred Barker's mutton-chop whiskers seemed to bristle at the

innuendo and he swiftly expressed his anger at the implication. "What the hell do you mean by that? We've pulled no wool over your eyes. We've been honest in our dealings. When you demanded due diligence, we opened up our books to you. We've played fair."

"Perhaps so, perhaps so," Leonard Charming soothed. But there was a malicious glint in his eye when he added, "But of course, it's often the case that some things are all out of our control, aren't they?"

"What's that supposed to mean?" Rick Barker asked tightly.

Leonard Channing managed to look vaguely unhappy. "Well, I happened to have an important lunch engagement at the Reform Club yesterday afternoon. A rather elderly, almost downmarket club these days, all sorts of rather raffish people seem to have joined it now, but it still has a certain decayed charm for me...However, in the course of conversation a comment was made that raised my interest. It led me to make certain other inquiries, among political friends of mine, and last evening...well, that's why I was unable to join you at the awards reception, Mr Hallam." His eyes met Eric's momentarily, and Eric caught the glimpse of deep satisfaction. "It seems that, as a result of the information I have received, I am no longer able to advise Mr Hallam that he should proceed with this purchase of Barker Marine. At least, not at the price that was put on the table, and which Barker Marine, fortunately, has still not seen fit to accept."

Hallam licked his lips; his eyes were hooded with surprise and he stared at the table. "What's this about, Channing?"

Channing sighed, the reluctant bearer of bad news for the Barker family. "While it is true that Mr Hallam has expressed reservations about the value of the defence contract, the projected profit levels were nevertheless taken into account when determining the price to be offered for Barker Marine. It now seems that price must be revised. Downwards."

"Why?" Fred Barker's voice cracked the silence, harsh as a pistol shot.

Channing raised an elegantly-suited shoulder, delicately,

deprecatingly. "Matters beyond our control, I'm afraid. The ...ah...people I spoke to last night confirmed the rumour I had picked up in the Reform Club. Our political masters have called for a review of all defence contracts: it seems defence cutbacks are in the offing. The news will break in the next week or so. Because of this, all defence contracts not yet commenced are to be suspended. The review is expected to take at least eight months. So..."

"There's no guarantee Barker Marine will get the contract they've been expecting," Hallam grated. "In that case—"

"In that case Martin and Channing could under no circumstances advise a continuation of the discussions as they presently stand. Guarantees are certainly not possible—the defence contract might never come our way, and even if it did, could not start until well after the purchase had been completed. So, as I said, a pig in a poke..."

"What exactly are you saying ?" Rick Barker asked in a dazed, almost defeated voice. Leonard Channing smiled thinly. "Absolutely no guarantees. And a withdrawal of the current offer. I have prepared a new one. We would now be recommending a price along these lines." He slid a piece of paper across to Fred Barker. The old man stared at it with mounting rage.

"This is a rip-off!" he exclaimed. "There's no way we could accept this kind of figure—"

"Martin and Channing would be advising Mr Hallam," Leonard Channing said in a soft but clinical tone, "that the price is not really negotiable any longer..."

"You mean, take it or leave it?" Fred Barker queried, with a rasp in his voice.

"Exactly so."

"That was really putting it to the old bastard!" Joe Hallam roared with delight and slapped Leonard Channing on the back. The chairman of Martin and Channing did not enjoy the congratulatory experience, but managed a wintry smile. He sipped gingerly at the celebratory malt whisky he had been offered in

Hallam's suite, high in the Newcastle building that gave a view of the sweep of the old Town Moor.

Eric stood by the window, looking out. In the far distance, a blurring sky gave the hint of rain. At Sedleigh Hall, near the Cheviot, it would probably already be raining. He felt the sudden, deep desire to get back there, to its clear, windswept hills, away from the city, from his own thoughts, and from Channing's grimy manoeuvrings with Hallam. He turned to look at Channing. "Was it really yesterday evening that you got that information?" he asked quietly.

Channing raised an eyebrow. "About the defence contracts? Come now, Eric, surely you don't disbelieve me? I assure you, there are rumours going the rounds..."

"Did you *start* them, Leonard?"

There was a short silence. Leonard Channing held Eric's glance for a while, then smiled, sipped his whisky. Joe Hallam stared at each of them in turn, sensing the dislike that crackled like electricity between them, his eyes wrinkling with suspicion. Then a broad grin spread over his craggy features. "Rumour? Am I getting this straight? What you said to the Barkers...it was just rumour? You mean you didn't *really* have a meeting last night with political friends?"

"I had dinner last night with *friends*," Channing admitted, "and we did talk about various things."

"You foxy bastard!" Hallam muttered admiringly.

"Things have been dragging on too long, Mr Hallam," Channing admonished in his chairman-severe tone. "The Barkers must be brought to heel. The financing of this project is a serious matter and cannot be held up longer by these emotional arguments from the vendors of the company. If I...exaggerated the likelihood of this review somewhat, well, so be it, but the end justifies the means. The Barkers are strapped for cash; they are living on their borrowings; they can't afford to wait to see whether what I've said is true—after all, any enquiries they make to the Ministry would be slow in response and could further jeopardize their position regarding the contract—and I see no reason why we should pay more for the assets than we need to. Than *you* need to, I should say."

"Lower price, lower commission to you, Channing," Hallam suggested maliciously.

"True, but a swifter return. Besides, a good job done now, to your advantage, would mean a possible entry to other of your future enterprises. Of which, I imagine, there will be more."

Hallam watched him for a moment, musingly, then nodded. "I think my backers will be favourably impressed."

"Who *are* your backers, Mr Hallam?" Eric asked.

Hallam assumed an air of indifference. "A syndicate. Interested in bringing life back to the river. In developing a seagoing facility right here, deep in the Tyne. And they'll be pleased that the price for a prime riverside site, where we can create a deep-sea anchorage, is to be lower than expected." He hesitated, eyeing Eric carefully. "But you don't seem greatly enamoured of the way things are going."

Eric shrugged. "I don't think the Barker demands were unreasonable. The guarantees really only amounted to peanuts, when you look at the general expenditure on the project. And I don't like Leonard's methods. But then, I never have."

"It's the principle," Hallam glowered. "I don't like getting screwed. Besides, since the defence contract will be delayed, or even killed—"

"We only have Leonard's word for that," Eric remarked quietly.

Hallam raised an eyebrow. "It's good enough for me. And if the story contains a certain…inaccuracy, well, it *was* described as a rumour, after all. Me, I approve of Leonard's initiative."

Channing smiled. "You should understand, Mr Hallam, Eric has always set himself up as a one-man conscience for the bank. Even though he sits on the board only as a non-executive director, appointed in a grace and favour situation. Mrs Ward, you see, holds a large percentage of Martin and Channing. He is actually his wife's appointee. Isn't that so, Eric?"

Eric refused to rise to the bait. After a few moments' amused scrutiny, Channing turned back to Hallam.

"However…did the reception go well last night?"

"I thought so. What do you reckon, Ward?"

Both men looked at him. There was a certain curiosity in Hallam's dark eyes as he stared at Eric; it raised new confusions in Eric's mind. He shrugged. "It went well enough, as far as I could make out."

"Eric's not exactly a party animal," Channing explained urbanely. "Even at his own home, Sedleigh Hall. But I'm sorry I was unable to be present. Was I missed?"

Hallam glanced at Channing; his eyes seemed to glitter a warning, quickly suppressed as he became aware of Eric's scrutiny. He laughed. "Hell, at a party like that, no one gets missed. I don't even know who was there altogether, or who they were with. And as for when people left, or who with, I wouldn't have the first idea. What time did *you* leave the shindig, Ward?"

Both men were looking at him, as though it were important. But Eric's mouth was dry.

He had crouched, stunned, staring horrified at the naked, lifeless body as it lay twisted in an unnatural position, locked now after the throes of an agonized death. His stomach was churning and the blood was pounding in his temples, his brain boiling with questions. He began to shiver, but for long seconds he was unable to gather his thoughts. Then finally the reason for his return to the flat came back to him, and he rose, stepped past the thing that had been Sandra Vitali and half-staggered into the bedroom.

The bedside light was switched on: he had left the room in darkness but she must have switched it on to go to the door. She must have heard the door buzzer, and assumed it was him, returning, maybe with a change of mind, wanting to continue the evening the way it had begun. She would have thrown open the door maybe, with a welcoming smile. And then…

He almost gagged. He had to concentrate…*concentrate.*

He cast around in the bathroom, and then began to search the rest of the room, looking desperately around the bed where they had discarded their clothes in an urgent passion that now seemed far away and obscene. Her own black dress and the silk panties she had worn were still there in a heap where he had thrown them. He remembered the feel of them as he had slipped them from her warm eager limbs but his gorge rose at the thought of touching them now.

With a gasp of relief he finally found what he was looking for. The keys were lying on the carpet, near the bedside table. He picked them up and the blood raged and pounded in his head. He put out a hand to steady himself, for he knew what was happening. In a moment it would come again, the old cat claws scratching at the back of his eyes, the violent pains racking him, the red blindness that would envelop him. The stress of the moment had overcome him. He reached into his pocket for the phial, but he already knew it wasn't there. There would be no immediate relief.

He lurched back into the sitting room. She lay there, accusingly. The pain seared at his nerve ends again and he wanted to get out of there, but he was unable to bear the sight of her sprawled, ruined nakedness and he went back to the bedroom. With trembling fingers he picked up the black dress that still lay crumpled on the bedroom floor and he came back to her, spread it over her, cloaking part of her twisted body, bringing back some kind of privacy, dignity to it.

Then he stumbled back into the hallway, back to the lift, back to the car. The stars glittered coldly at him as his nerve ends screamed. He unlocked the car, lurched into the driving seat and scrabbled for the emergency phial he kept in the glove compartment, laid his head back on the seat, allowed the fluid to drip into his eyes.

But in his mind he could still see the blackened face of the woman who had been beautiful, the woman he had made love to, only a short while ago…

2

Charlie Spate was not a happy man.

The first thing was, he had still not come to terms with his removal to Tyneside: to him it was a retrograde step, away from the London haunts he knew so well. And he had little but contempt for the men he was forced to work with in the North: he regarded them as clod-hopping, unimaginative, and unsophisticated. At the same time he resented the politics that had driven him here: the investigations into the Fraud Squad activities had not affected him directly, other than the matter of those two women, and yet it had been felt best to remove some of the key players in the detective force, reassign them to other duties. When he had protested, there had been a few phone calls and a brutal choice.

He had chosen the lesser of two evils. As a result he was stuck in the North.

And now, within a matter of weeks, he had a really messy one, with no personal contacts he could make, no snouts he could pick up information from, just a reliance on men and women he didn't know and didn't rate. He prowled around the room again, watching the scene of crime unit at work. The body of the woman had already been zipped up in the body bag, now that the pathologist had finished his early examination. As usual, he had had little to impart: they were always cagey buggers, Spate considered. One thing the pathologist had advised, though: "Take care of the bedsheets. I think we might find she'd engaged in sexual activity shortly before death. Just a hunch."

Hunch. It was bloody obvious from the state of the bedroom. The woman naked, with a broken neck, lying just inside the open door of her apartment. What was it, a quarrel after her lover had stuck it to her? A killer with a sick sense of humour, anyway, Charlie Spate considered, draping her black dress over the corpse after snapping the life from her body.

Or maybe a remorseful killer: there had been a phone message, from an unidentified caller, telling the police where the killing had occurred.

But it wasn't just this that left him unhappy. He called a conference of the unit in his office three days after the discovery of the body and expressed his unhappiness.

He stood in front of them, a lean man of middle height with

a mouth like bent iron and nervous hands. "I got a bad feeling about this one. Too many things I don't understand; too many loose ends. There's a load of questions come up, but none of you have raised any answers as yet. And it's been three days. The longer it takes, the colder the trail gets." He didn't add that the Chief Constable was already on his back. The press he could deal with—tell them to shove off. Although, apparently, one didn't talk to the local press like that. So the Chief Constable advised. He glared around at the silent group in front of him. "So, talk to me. What've we got so far?"

The detective constable sitting in front of him seemed somewhat nervous. He glanced at his colleagues and cleared his throat. "Well, we still don't have a clear idea of the dead woman's identity. We turned up three different passports in the apartment, in the names of Maureen Collins, Sandra Vitali, and Jean O'Hara. We've checked with the passport office but they reckon all the documents were forged."

"Which tells us what?" Spate demanded.

The constable shrugged. "Criminal activity?" he ventured.

"And some," Spate said, his grey eyes glittering with contempt. "For God's sake, people don't have three different passports if they're not involved in *some* villainy. Question is, what and why? She has no record on Tyneside?"

Detective Sergeant Perry, heavy, stolid, gloomy of manner, shook his greying head. "She's not known to us; not under any of those names. But from the clothing in her wardrobe...my guess is she's a traveller all right, London, overseas, and regular. Whatever she was up to, it was extensive and well paid."

"Like the apartment," the woman suggested. She was a detective constable—Elaine Start, he understood she was called. She had sturdy legs, and the kind of figure that would have led more than a few stallions on the force to try her out, he guessed. If he hadn't been wiser, he might even have been tempted himself, but after that bit of business in the Met...

"Expensive tastes," Detective Constable Start went on, "recently decorated apartment, the rental paid in advance, well-stocked wardrobe..."

"Who paid the rental?" Spate demanded.

There was a silence, the small group of officers facing him looking somewhat sheepish. Spate sighed. "All right," he said wearily, "let's go over it again. We got a woman with three identities, three passports obtained illegally. She's living in a flat with the rent paid up in advance but we don't know her boyfriend—assuming it *was* a boyfriend who stumped up the cash. So, item number one, find the rent payer."

Detective Constable Start scribbled in her notebook.

"Next, we need to find out how she made a living. It may be she was on the game, but if so it was likely high class. She's got no record on Tyneside. What the press are already calling a mystery woman. We don't know what her job was—though as I say, we can guess at its nature. So, item two—what was she up to here in Newcastle?"

He paused, eyeing the group dispiritedly. "We know nothing about her in general terms. But we do know how she was killed. Yes?"

Detective Sergeant Perry brightened. He was feeling out of his depth, but this gave him a chance. "Broken neck," he offered.

Spate remained calm. "Not just that. There was no sign of a great fight. It was a professional job. Half throttled, and then a quick twist, arm against the throat, hand on the back of the head. Forensic may give us more later. Then there's the next item: someone called in, told us there'd been a killing. So, who would do that? A casual passer-by? Hardly. And why? Was it the killer or someone else? Meanwhile, what else can we surmise?"

There was a long silence. Patiently, Spate suggested, "Let's take this for starters. The woman is in bed. Naked. She hears the doorbell. She walks through to the door, opens it and this guy steps in, grabs her by the throat before she can raise a shout, and in seconds, as she's blacking out, he completes the job with a quick snap. Then, because he takes some kind of pleasure in showing us the finger, he even rings in to tell us what's happened. Now where are the holes in all that?"

The female detective constable hesitated. "A woman wouldn't normally respond that way, to a caller late at night."

"How do you mean?"

"She'd dress—put on a dressing gown or something, before she opened the door. And for that matter, she wouldn't open the door at all without checking the identity of her visitor. Unless..."

"What?"

"Unless she knew who it was. Maybe, was already expecting him."

"Naked?"

Elaine Start had calm eyes that were not easily disturbed. "If she knew the man, standing there naked to greet him like that, it could have been a deliberate turn-on...you know, ready for her lover..."

The eyes were dark brown, steady, and yet challenging. Spate wondered about that look—it reminded him of someone. Then as the men in the group shuffled a little, one or two sniggering uneasily at her imagery, he nodded, somewhat mollified. "If that was the case, she certainly didn't get the response she expected. And then, what about the black dress?"

"Sir?"

"It was draped over her. Why?"

Detective Constable Start tapped a thoughtful pencil against her lips. Charlie Spate considered there was a certain sensuality about that mouth. He waited. "It would suggest concern," she suggested.

"I thought at first maybe it was just a sick joke," Spate muttered, after a short silence, "but maybe you're not far off. Thing is, why would a man who had killed a woman be concerned about her nakedness after she was dead?"

" Sexual jealousy?"

"Go on," Spate said, interested at the thought.

She wrinkled her slightly freckled snub nose. "If this was a crime of passion, you know—maybe she'd been two-timing her lover, he goes round, kills her, but then still feels enough not to want to have her seen by all and sundry, naked the way she is...a sort of scenario like that, perhaps..." Her voice trailed away uncertainly as she became aware of the way the men were staring at her.

"Sounds like we got a real kink here," the detective sergeant grumbled. Spate glared at Perry in annoyance; he had already decided who he wanted to help him on this particular investigation. In case anything else came up and the investigating team was narrowed—as no doubt it would be. It would not involve Detective Sergeant Perry: he was already out of his league. Start was different, if somewhat female in her fancies. Or maybe her woman's point of view held more sense than they all presently credited her for.

"All right, Start, I want you to get around the other people in those apartments. I know we've interviewed them already, but this time I want the woman's touch." He was unable to keep the slight sneer out of his tone, and she flushed slightly. "The dead woman was no saint—I'll bet my bottom dollar there'll be some in that building who had views about her and the company she kept. I want you to find out—"

He was interrupted by the jangling of the phone on his desk. He picked it up in some irritation, barked his name and then listened. When he replaced the phone he was silent for a little while. Then he took a deep breath, "All right, as you were. It seems troubles don't come singly in this God-forsaken part of the world. We got another one."

"Another murder?" the detective sergeant asked in surprise.

"Seems like. But this time, we got someone caught on the premises, which is something, ain't it? And as for the woman in the black dress, it seems a car has turned up, which looks as though it could be linked to her. The Gosforth Park hotel staff reported it as left in their car park for the last few days, unclaimed, unattended. It's been checked out. A registration, in the name of Sandra Vitali. Looks like we got our first breakthrough—let's hope it leads to bigger things." He rose to his feet, decisively. "So, young woman, you're coming with me. You others, I want one of you down to supervise the checking of that car—every damned inch of it before the clodhoppers who found it trash every useful sign there is there; and you two talk to the hotel staff, find out what the car was doing there in the first instance. You," he added, staring at the detective sergeant, "you can get on with chasing up the forensic science lab. We want some answers quickly, not next week, so use whatever muscle you got with the liaison officer to get some information out of that lab before we all join Sandra Vitali, out of bloody boredom!"

The Chief Constable was a big man, with a deliberately military bearing. He was reputed to have been a hard one in his early days in the West Midlands, a failed law undergraduate who'd found his forte in the discipline of the police, He'd spent some time in the Met, before progressing up the ladder to reach the top on Tyneside. There was a vague Welsh accent to be discerned from time to time, but not always: it was as though he wished it to be known that he had not forgotten his roots, even though most of the time he ignored them.

"So, DCI, settling in, then?"

"More or less, sir," Charlie Spate replied.

"It'll take a while, of course, I quite understand. And there are things to put behind you. The inquiries at the Met…they exonerated you, of course—"

"I was never actually under suspicion, sir," Spate snapped.

"Of course, of course," the Chief Constable replied hurriedly, a little irritated. "But I'll tell you frankly, so that we're all under no illusions, I wasn't terribly happy to take you on as a DCI here, with your record—"

"Sir?"

The Chief Constable stared at him hard. "I don't think we want to go too closely into the instances of your insubordination, Spate, the talk about the two prostitutes, the suspicions that you were involved too closely with certain undesirable people—"

"They were police informants, sir."

"Yes. Well." The Chief Constable cleared his throat. "That's all in the bygones. It's on your record, but you'll not hear me refer to it again. Clean slate, hey?" His smile was insincere, his heartiness forced. He moved on with the dismissive smoothness of a bigot. "Now then, since you got here things have got busy, haven't they? Busy enough to keep you out of mischief, I'd guess."

Charlie Spate subdued his anger. He didn't have to take this, he thought; then he reminded himself that maybe he did. The Met was gone as far as he was concerned: he still had his rank. It was best to play along for the moment. He remained silent.

The Chief Constable eyed him carefully. "As I say, you arrive, and so do the killings. We now have two, I understand."

"Yes sir."

"Talk to me."

Charlie Spate took a deep breath. "I've already sent you an interim briefing paper on the Vitali murder. We're now following up on the car, and we're talking to the staff at the hotel. Seems like she may well have been there at some kind of reception."

The Chief Constable raised his head like a predator scenting game. "Reception?"

Spate nodded. "I don't have all the details yet, but there was some kind of shindig at the hotel the night Vitali died. So we'll need to get hold of a guest list, interview everyone who was present—"

"Yes," the Chief Constable muttered vaguely. His glance did not meet Spate's. "Once you have that list, let me see it. Before you start talking to the people named."

Spate raised his eyebrows. The Chief Constable said no more, giving no explanation, but Spate could guess. Swish hotel, reception, maybe some important people there. Chief Constables moved in high circles, needed to make sure the feathers of the birds they flew with didn't get ruffled. Unnecessarily.

"What about this other killing?"

Spate hesitated. "We got calls about a bit of a battle up at this apartment. Beat coppers got there first. No body to be found in the apartment, but blood everywhere."

The Chief Constable was puzzled. "So how come there's talk of murder?"

"They found someone at the bottom of the stairs, outside the flat. He was high, apparently. Babbled about murder. Confused, crazy. So they locked him up, till he got himself together. So, no corpse, buckets of blood, flat looked like a riot took place, and a guy with a broken arm and veins pumped full of smack talking his head off. Then, at least."

"So you think the owner of the flat's been murdered?"

"And disposed of. Looks like, sir."

"You know who lived at the flat?"

Charlie Spate nodded. He watched the Chief Constable carefully. He'd noted other reactions to the name. "Yes, sir. A man called Sam Cullen."

The Chief Constable grimaced, and sucked his teeth. He was silent for a little while. Then he nodded. "Looks like we're going to have trouble on our hands, DCI. I'll need bulletins on this one, as well. The man you have in custody…you say he's talking?"

"*Was* talking, sir."

"And now?"

"He wants to see his lawyer."

3

The narrow interview room was shabby and confined: a small table, badly scarred with cigarette burns, two chairs, grim, grey-painted walls that suggested a determination to give no comfort to prisoners, and a narrow window that was grimy and fly-specked. Eric had seen rooms like this a hundred times during his years with the police: he did not seem to have progressed much in his life, he thought to himself. Nothing much had changed in twenty years.

He stared at the man facing him. Tramline Stevens was not a happy man. He was smoking a cigarette but his hand was trembling and he was unable to control the quick, darting movements of his eyes, unable to settle his glance, ill at ease, uncertain and panicky. One side of his face was marked with a deep purple bruise that had half closed one eye; his arm was in a sling, and he was decidedly in a bad physical state.

"So whose fault was it this time, Mr Stevens?" Eric asked caustically. "You going to claim police brutality?"

Stevens looked even more alarmed. "Now I'm not saying that,

Mr Ward. I'm in enough trouble as it is—I don't want to get the fuzz turning really nasty on me as well." He dragged shakily at his cigarette. "No, this batterin', it all happened before they got there."

Wearily, Eric suggested, "I think you'd better tell me the whole story."

"I was set up, Mr Ward!"

"Again? Just as you were over Gilsland? Seems to be the story of your life."

"But it's the truth, you got to believe me! I'm a very unlucky man, Mr Ward. Life isn't treating me right!"

He sounded most aggrieved. Eric observed him dispassionately for a few moments and then shrugged. "All right, you'd better tell me all about it."

Stevens hesitated, his cheek twitching spasmodically. He inspected the end of his cigarette and licked his lips. "Well, you know, this Gilsland thing's been gettin' me down, Mr Ward. I know you're on my case now, and I expect you'll get to the truth, but I was down, like, and I needed...well, you know...Anyway, my credit's not too good around the town, and I was gettin' desperate."

"And?"

"I went looking for some stuff. But I swear to you, I didn't know I was goin' to get involved in no murder!"

"You were found at the scene. Is that where you went for the drugs?"

"No, that's not the way it was at all. At the apartment, when I came to...well, I don't remember too much about it, honest! When the polis arrived I was sort of out of my skull, you know what I mean? I'd taken some stuff, you see—"

"Not at the apartment?"

"No. Earlier."

"When?"

"About a half hour earlier. Then I went around to this place—"

"Why did you go there? To meet someone?"

"Naw, it wasn't like that," Stevens replied miserably. "You see, like I told you, I was gettin' desperate to get hold of some stuff and I finally found this guy who let me have some—but I had to do somethin' for him in return."

"And what was that?"

"I had to deliver a message."

"Go on."

"Well, I agreed, and I went around to the address he gave me, and he told me there'd probably not be anyone in and I was to wait until someone turned up and I was to give the message to him. But there was no lights on in the place and I waited around in the street for a while, and then I saw someone go in, and I waited a bit longer and I thought I'd go on up there. And that's when it all fell apart."

"What happened?"

"It's all a but hazy, like; I mean, with the fact I was a bit high and all that, but I went in from the street with this message and that's when it all happened." He shook his head mournfully. "The polis are saying I killed somebody, but that's not my style, Mr Ward. I'm small beer, me. And they're saying if it wasn't me, I was in on it, but I swear to you—"

"Never mind swearing," Eric interposed. "Just tell me what you remember."

Tramline Stevens stubbed out his cigarette on the table top as many others had done before him. He shook his head. "It was all confused. I went into the place, I started climbing up the stairs. It was all quiet. I thought I'd just stick the message under the door, you know what I mean? I was supposed to give it to the guy, you know, but everything was dark. And then, when I got to the stop of the stairs everything happened all at once. This big guy, the door opened and he came out of the apartment, someone slung over his shoulder and he sort of looked at me and then he kind of went berserk. I mean I wasn't doin nothin'—I was there on an innocent errand, but it was like he went crazy. He sort of threw this guy at me, then launched himself at me. I went arse over tip, bouncin' right down the stairs and he came after me like a tiger, I tell you. I remember him hitting me when I was sort of kneelin' at the foot of the stairs..." He lifted a finger, delicately stroked the outline of the bruise on his face. "And the bastard kicked me too, a couple of times. In the ribs. I can show you the bruises."

Eric declined the opportunity. "And your arm?"

"I think that was a kick too." Stevens shook his head in wonderment. "I don't know how I'm still alive."

"Did you know the man who attacked you?"

Stevens shook his head mournfully. "I only caught a quick look at him. He was a big bugger, I'll tell you that. But it all happened so quick. I don't think I'd recognise him again."

"What happened to the message you were carrying? Do you still have it?"

"I don't know what happened to it. Sure, I ain't got it now. Maybe that big bugger took it."

If there was a message at all, Eric considered. "So you wouldn't know who attacked you, and you no longer have the message—your reason for going there...Did you know who lived in the apartment?"

Stevens squirmed uneasily. "Look, I was just there to deliver a message."

"So you say. But the man who lived there was Sam Cullen. Well known in the Tyneside underworld. And now he doesn't seem to be around any more. You were found there, babbling about murder—"

"I was out of my head, Mr Ward!"

"You were talking about murder, Cullen's missing, there are signs of disorder in the apartment...and you were there just to deliver a message."

"That's the honest truth, Mr Ward."

"What was the message about?"

"I don't know. It was a note. I didn't read it."

"Who gave it to you?"

"I don't know. I seen him around a few times, but I don't know his name."

Eric sighed. "If you don't tell me the whole story, how do you expect me to help you?"

Tramline Stevens showed his desperation in his eyes. "Look, Mr Ward, I swear to you, it's the truth as much as I can remember.

I wanted a fix but none of my regular dealers would help me out. I didn't have the money, and maybe they've been warned off anyway, because of the Gilsland thing and word on the street. But I kept askin' around and in the end I came across this kid...I knew he did some tradin' from time to time, but he wasn't one of my regular suppliers. So I don't know his name. I could recognize him if I saw him again," he added eagerly.

"And he gave you a message for Sam Cullen."

"That's it, that's it. He'd give me a fix; I'd take the message."

"Why couldn't he take it himself?"

Stevens shrugged. "I didn't ask. All I wanted was a fix. So we did the deal. He gave me a snort, I went around to Cullen's place. And that's how it all went down."

"The police think you're part of a gangland killing," Eric said quietly.

"Aw, come on Mr Ward..." Stevens replied miserably.

They were both silent for a while. Eric took a deep breath. "It all sounds shaky to me, but...I think the police are also grasping at straws. There's no body, nothing to link you to Cullen. All they have is you on the premises, signs of a disturbance, Cullen missing...You sure there's nothing else you have to tell me?"

"That's the whole story, Mr Ward. You'll help me?"

Eric shrugged. "As far as I can."

The problem was he felt unable to concentrate on anything at the moment. He was still racked with feelings of personal guilt and his mind sill swirled with the memory of the scene he had left the other evening—the woman, naked, on the floor...He shook his head, and rose to his feet. "All right, Mr Stevens, I'll start some enquiries, find out what we can on the street. But I stress to you—you'd better be telling me the truth...and all of it."

Tramline Stevens seemed pathetically grateful.

Eric left the room and walked down the corridor. He passed a couple of uniformed policemen: they looked at him warily. They recognised him, knew he had once been one of them. But now as far as they were concerned he was on the other side of the fence. One of the enemy.

He reached out to push back the swing doors that led from

the corridor to the reception area. He paused as his name was called. He turned. The man walking towards him was unfamiliar. He was of medium height and stocky, hair cut short; his pugnacious chin emphasized his aggressive manner. He had the air and certainty of a man who was determined to get results. "You're Eric Ward."

"That's right."

"I'm Charlie Spate. DCI."

"We've not met before."

"That's right. And you're acting for that ratbag Stevens."

"Mr Stevens is my client, yes," Eric replied coolly.

"You know we got him bang to rights, don't you?"

"I hardly think so."

"Ha, he's just low life, is Tramline Stevens. I'm surprised a man like you would bother acting for him. He's a loser. We've got him over the Gilsland matter, and now we're going to tie him into something more serious. This has got all the hallmarks of a gangland vendetta, Ward...and I guess you know enough about that kind of thing from your own experience."

"People have been talking."

Charlie Spate snorted. "Don't they always? As for Stevens, we want our little sparrow in there to sing, and then maybe we'll cut some kind of deal with him. We don't think he's a main mover in this, but he's involved all right, and we'll nail him, unless he has the sense to cooperate."

Eric smiled contemptuously.

"Nail him for what? Substance abuse? Being hospitalized by an unknown assailant?"

"Witness to, and participant in a murder."

"You're a long way from proving that," Eric replied. "Anyway, if you'll excuse me..."

He pushed his way through the swing doors and headed for the main entrance. He was aware of Charlie Spate following him. As he stepped into the street he heard the door open behind him. He glanced back: Spate was standing in the doorway, staring at him.

"Is there something else?" Eric asked. His mouth was dry

suddenly. He felt as though Spate knew something about the dead woman, saw him as a potential suspect, was playing with him. It was an irrational feeling, but it was an anxiety he could not quell.

Charlie Spate nodded slowly. "Yes…You fancy a drink?"

Chapter three

1

The public bar of the George and Dragon was crowded, so Spate muscled his way through the throng and they entered the lounge bar, which was quieter. They managed to find some seats in a corner alcove: Spate left Eric there while he went to the bar to order some drinks.

When he came back with Eric's lager and a pint of Special for himself he sat down, and grimaced. "There's one thing you can say for the North, anyway: the beer's good."

"So I'm told," Eric said quietly. "So?"

He waited. He was still not certain why he had agreed to join Spate in the George and Dragon. It was an unusual situation, and one he would normally not have agreed to. But he was curious: he wondered what had motivated Spate to invite him. And overlying the curiosity was the shadow of his anxieties: he was still unable to get out of his mind the image of Sandra Vitali sprawled on the carpet. He wondered what Charlie Spate knew...or had guessed.

"Cheers!" Spate said and grinned, took a long draught of his beer and set the glass down. "I needed that."

Eric observed him for a few seconds, and then said, "So?"

"So what?"

"This is a bit out of the ordinary. Solicitor, and investigating officer. Socializing."

Spate's grin widened. "That's all it is. Socializing. I'm a copper. You're an ex-copper. I just felt maybe we had things in common. So, it's just socializing."

Eric did not believe him. Charlie Spate would have something else on his mind. "No. I can't accept that."

Spate shrugged. His smile faded, the good humour fading like a gaslight turning down. He frowned slightly, and inspected his beer glass with exaggerated care. His tone was impassive. "I been asking around about you, as soon as I heard you were representing Tramline Stevens. What are you doing with low-life like him?"

"It's a living."

Charlie Spate looked at him: there was uncertainty in his glance. "Like I said, I been asking around about you. The story is you were a good copper. Then you got problems…with your eyes."

"It's well enough known."

"So you had to pack it in. But…so they say, you were lucky. You married well."

Eric looked at him, betraying nothing in the impassivity of his features. Charlie Spate watched him for a few moments and then smiled suddenly in genuine, if somewhat malicious amusement. "You bug people, you know that? They can't fix you, can't put you into a category. I've asked around, and they all say the same thing. What the hell's with that character? He's got a problem with his eyes; he marries a rich woman; he's got into the corporate world of high finance; what's he doing running a crummy practice down on the Quayside, working for peanuts?"

"Maybe it's what I'm most comfortable doing," Eric suggested.

"Naw, I don't think it's that." Charlie Spate sipped his beer reflectively. "I think you know exactly who you are, exactly what you are, and you don't give a damn what people think about you. I like that. So that's why I thought maybe you and I ought to have a drink."

"Because I know who I am?" Eric asked ironically.

"Because I think we have things in common, because everyone reckons you're straight—and because I'm the new boy around here, and you know a hell of a sight more about Tyneside and its villains than I do. From both sides of the fence."

"You're not telling me you need help?" Eric asked.

Charlie Spate did not care for the mocking tone in Eric's voice. He bridled, glowered somewhat. "Hey, I'm putting out compliments here."

Eric was still wary: he still did not trust the man facing him across the table. He had not lost the occupational suspicion that had served him well on the force, in the old days. "I don't need them. What do you want, exactly?"

Spate stared at his drink and was silent for a little while. Then he shrugged slightly. "Actually, it's really like I said, I just wanted a drink with someone I thought I could talk to. Because I've had my problems too. I didn't want to come up here to this God-forsaken hole, I had a career in the Smoke, and I knew where I was. But, a few errors—which I admit—a few misconceptions, and I get saddled with the sins of others as well as my own. So here I am. Somewhat pissed off. And I just thought, after what I heard about you, maybe we had something in common. Like…a common integrity. A common cross to bear, A common inclination to tell the world to go to hell. Or maybe it's just that I don't like drinking alone. Take your pick."

Eric stared at him. He recognized the surliness in Spate's tone for what it was. It seemed there probably was no hidden agenda of the kind Eric had suspected. It was just that Charlie Spate felt isolated. He was suddenly relieved, and somewhat angry with himself. He had been so on edge, so concerned with his own problems he hadn't taken the invitation at face value. He leaned forward, picked up his drink. "Well, as you said, the beer isn't all that bad."

After a moment, Charlie Spate grunted. "Yeah. Well. To hell with it. So is your client guilty?"

"Of what?"

Charlie Spate shrugged and looked around the lounge. "I don't know. His story sounds crackers. But it could be true. But it was *Sam Cullen* who got whacked up there…You must know about Cullen."

Eric nodded. "I remember him years ago when he was starting out. A tearaway. Good-looking, rough, muscle and brain, not your usual product of the West End. He soon got over the heavy, image-building violence and settled down—if that's the right phrase—to making a career for himself. He's never been inside, because he's clever, but it's well enough known that he's built a pretty solid business for himself along the river."

"That's what I hear." Charlie Spate paused. "But let's not make any hero out of this character. What's the story of recent years?"

Eric considered the matter for a little while. "Cullen's never had any principles. He always went where the money was. There was a time when he ran the one-arm bandits; then he branched out into prostitution. But that's behind him now...of recent years...the street says he's been behind a lot of the soft drugs that have come into the market. And maybe some of the heavier stuff too."

"Setting up something like that needs money," Spate considered. "Who's been backing this boy?"

"There's been plenty of backing, but the source isn't known on the street. To all intents and purposes, Sam Cullen was the number one."

"So you still got connections along the river," Spate suggested, eyeing him appraisingly. "That could be useful: we could maybe do some work together. So this Cullen's been around a while."

"And active."

"But never pinned down." Spate's voice was soft. "I've seen it all before, of course. The tearaway gets sorted out; gets some backing and builds an organization, sets up a network. But that causes ripples...there are always rivals out there. And this...event...it has all the signs of a hit. Cullen's been removed. Which means that whoever arranged that, did it in order to step into vacant shoes."

Eric stared at him thoughtfully. "You think this is the beginning of some kind of drugs war?

"Like I said—I've seen it before."

"And Tramline Stevens?"

Spate shrugged noncommittally. "Hell, I don't know. Small fry. He's caught up in it somehow, but I'm not clear about all that. We're going to hold him of course, and make him sweat, till we make sure he's giving us all he's got. But I don't see him as a major player in this thing: I think he got caught up, maybe in the way he tells it. A dealer, one of Cullen's own, trying to warn of the hit he's got wind of in the street, unwilling to use the phone or reach out himself, sending a shambles like Tramline

Stevens…hell, I never thought I'd be talking like this to the brief who's looking after the villain's interests."

Eric smiled. "I take your point."

Charlie Spate looked at him, curiosity shading his eyes. "I just don't feel you're on their side, you know? The way many of you lawyers are. Working the system, even though they know their clients are guilty as hell."

"It's not quite like that," Eric replied carefully. "There's a duty—"

"I know, I know," Spate said gloomily. "Lawyers are independent; you make no judgements; you speak for your client, and your own views about possible guilt are irrelevant. I've heard it all. Anyway, I didn't come here to milk you about your client. Let's leave Tramline Stevens and the murder of a small drugs czar for the moment. What the hell do you call a small drugs czar, anyway?"

'Dead?"

Spate laughed. "Okay, I'll buy that one." He finished his drink, and agreed to another. When Eric came back to the table with the single glass he raised his eyebrows. "You not partaking?"

"I go canny with alcohol. Not making a point…constitution."

Spate nodded sympathetically. "You still get trouble."

"Occasionally." Eric felt a coldness creep into his blood as he said it. The memory of the attack he had suffered the other night came back to him; the shuddering, the pain that clawed at him; the inability to cope with the events that faced him; the illogical, spasmodic reactions—and here he was, talking with the man who would be investigating the events of that night. The man who could ruin his career and his marriage.

"There was another reason for wanting to have a chat with you," Spate was saying, casually. "When I heard Stevens wanted you to represent him, I asked around. Got the background on you. Then your name came up in another context as well."

"What was that?" Eric asked in a guarded tone.

"Hell, it never rains but it pours. You might have heard we have two killings on our hands. It's not just the murder of Sam Cullen, and the spiriting away of his corpse—why the hell would they do that anyway? Were they hoping there'd be no follow-up? Stevens maybe stumbled in on that and spoiled that particular idea...Anyway," he added in a spasm of irritability, "forget that. There's the girl, as well."

Fear stirred and stretched in Eric's stomach like a yawning tiger. "Girl?"

"She was called—among other things—Sandra Vitali. She was careless enough to get her neck snapped a few nights ago. And your name came up."

Eric forced himself to stay calm. Quietly, he asked, "My name came up? In what context? What exactly do you mean?"

Charlie Spate wrinkled his nose. "Nothing to get worried about. There's no thought that *you* whacked her! Respectable solicitor, ex-copper and all that! Though there's a few women I've felt like whacking in my time...No, it's just that we nosed around her flat and found she had three passports. Expensive flat, but no leads. Then it turns out she left her car at the Gosforth Park Hotel. So, naturally, we check the staff to find out what she might have been doing there. And we discover there was a reception there the night she died. And it seems she was present. Lot of people there. We got a list. Your name was on it—naturally, it sort of leapt out at me when you walked in with Stevens. Did you know her? This Sandra Vitali?"

"Why do you ask?" Eric's tone was defensive.

Spate raised his eyebrows. "Hey, this isn't any court of law! I was just asking—it's just that your name's on that list. We'll be talking to everyone on it. You know the way these things work. You were there; she was there. I just wondered. Had you ever come across her before?"

Eric shook his head. "No. Never heard of her. Never met her." That much at least was true—before that night.

"Did you see her there, at the reception?"

Eric shrugged. His blood was cold. "I didn't know her, can't say..."

"Apparently there was some kind of scene at one point. She belted someone. I still haven't fixed what it was all about, and the guy involved is on business in Spain, it seems, but did you—"

"I seem to recall there was an altercation...a young blonde, good-looking woman, slapped a middle-aged man. I got the impression maybe he'd made an unwelcome approach. She got pulled away...it was over in seconds."

Spate sighed. "That'll have been her. I don't suppose you happened to talk to her at the reception?"

"No." Eric hesitated. "I spent most of the time with an old acquaintance—ex-DCI Sampson."

Spate pulled a face. "Ah. The guy I replaced. It's a small world." He was silent for a little while. "He wasn't too sore about me coming in, I hope."

"He was happy enough to retire. And he picked up a good job."

"Head of security at the hotel, I hear."

"That's right." The tension in Eric's muscles began to fade, as they moved away from the topic that bothered him. But the relief was short-lived.

Sampson was there on duty, I suppose."

"He calmed things down. But I don't think he spoke to the girl, either."

Spate grimaced, shook his head. "The people we've spoken to so far, none of them admit to knowing her, now she's dead. That's what death means sometimes. No one ever remembers you." He brooded on the thought for a little while, as Eric sat silently, still tense. "Anyway...I guess, if you didn't speak to Sandra Vitali that night, you wouldn't know what she was doing there."

"No, I wouldn't know. I saw her, but...she seemed generally unattached."

"I wonder who the hell invited her there...who she was with."

"It's possible she was alone."

"Beautiful woman like that? I doubt it. Someone invited her; someone probably met her. It's sure as hell someone took her home. She'd made her own way to the function, but she took a lift back to her apartment—from someone."

"How do you know that?"

"Because she left her car at the hotel."

Eric thought it best to keep silent.

"Right. But we're interviewing everyone. We'll hit the jackpot in the end. We'll talk to everyone who was there."

"The way you're talking to me." Eric managed to keep his tone calm, jocular, in spite of the painful pounding of blood in his temples.

"You think this is an interview? Hell no," Spate laughed. "This is just a chat in the pub. We'll get around to a formal statement from you later. We've got the list, we're working through it, alphabetically, would you believe—your turn will come. But I just wondered, since we were talking over a drink, and you were there that night..."

"Have you come up with any theories about her...death?" Eric asked with a forced casualness.

Spate shook his head ruefully. "I got a female detective constable who thinks it was maybe a crime of passion. But there's the passports. And who paid for the apartment? And then there was the car..."

"What about the car?" Eric asked, maintaining his casual tone, the disinterested observer.

Spate frowned. "Well, she left it at the hotel car park. Now that wasn't surprising, in itself. she'd had plenty to drink, and she could have left it because she was incapable of driving. But when we took a look at it we realized she left it because it wouldn't start. So she must have got a lift home, because she was killed a couple of hours later in her own apartment. But then there's another thing...someone rang in, didn't leave a name, but told the sergeant on duty that there'd been a killing. Then rang off. Someone who clearly didn't want to be involved. But the passports, the broken neck—a professional job, believe me—the phone call, the draping of a dress over the body, I tell you, at this stage nothing seems to be hanging together. And then again, there's the car..."

"You said earlier...it wouldn't start." Eric's mouth was dry.

Spate nodded, his eyes reflective. "Yes, that's right. But it's the reason *why* it wouldn't start that interests me. You see, Sandra Vitali must have come out of that reception alone—a couple of people say that there were some passes made at the bar but she rejected them and made her way to the car park alone. Then, when she got down to her car, it wouldn't start. At that point, someone picked her up and drove her home. My guess is, it was her killer."

Eric felt as though Charlie Spate must have heard the thunder of his blood. "Why do you make that assumption?"

"Stands to reason. The fact is the car wouldn't start because it had been tampered with: some of the wiring had been ripped out, quickly and crudely." He looked at Eric and smiled. "Simple, isn't it? You disable a car. You wait until your target comes out, can't get the bloody thing started. And then you stroll up, knight in shining armour. Give her a lift home. And then you pop her. Yes, I think if we can find out who gave her that lift home, we'll know who whacked her." He shook his head. "But this guy made a bad mistake."

Eric's pulse was beating hard. He forced himself to sip at his lager, controlling the shaking of his hand, aware that there were claws reaching for him again, threatening to start the scratching at the back of his eyes. "Mistake?"

"She was a beautiful woman," Charlie Spate mused. "I've known a few in my time: it's been one of my weaknesses, women. Believe me. But our friend, he disabled her car, he took her home, and she was grateful. So, he thought he might as well take what was on offer before he finished what he'd set out to do."

"What do you mean?" Eric asked, his tongue rasping against the roof of his mouth.

Spate grinned unpleasantly. "This guy, before he whacked her, he screwed her. He laid her in her own little bed, then when she took him to the door to say goodnight he did the deed. It was quick. A last, fatal embrace, you might say. He broke her pretty neck, neat, quick, professional. But it wasn't very professional of him to screw her."

Eric said nothing. He was staring fixedly at his half-empty glass.

"Forensic have come up with the goods," Spate announced cheerfully. "They found traces of semen at the post-mortem. It was from a recent event, not long before death. And it was from consensual sex: young Sandra hadn't been unenthusiastic about it. So, if it was someone at the reception who fixed her car, took her home, and screwed her before doing what he'd intended to do all along, we should be able to fix him. We would probably have been able to find something, flakes of skin, fingerprints, whatever...but this makes it much easier. Semen. It's just a matter of going through the whole list of fifty-plus guys, taking hair samples, and checking the DNA. At least, it should be that simple." He grinned at Eric, triumphantly. "So, we're working on it. Your time will come my friend, count on it. We'll get around to you too, to get the complete picture. I mean, we can't leave any stones unturned, can we?"

2

Somewhere along towards the bend of the river an owl called, distant, eerie, echoing the lonely hooting of a sea-bound tug, ploughing doggedly past the freighters moored at Pandon. Wisps of fog twisted wraithlike shapes above the dark water that lapped against the Quayside, dim ghost lights gleaming and flickering in the misty late February evening air. There was no breeze along the river and no sound other than the rumble of traffic along the vaguely outlined, mist-shrouded shape of the Tyne Bridge above his head. Eric shivered slightly as he locked up the office, before turning to make his way along the echoing quayside, up Dog Leap Stairs, to enter Gray Street and turn into the narrow entry that led to the Old Market.

He had not been sleeping well. He had stayed in Gosforth for several nights now, busy during the day, tortured with conscience, guilt and anxiety shredding the night hours. Sedleigh Hall seemed a world away, and though he longed to return to its peace something kept him away, as though if he went back there now he would have to face an echoing loneliness, an isolation, and the brutal realities of his recent behaviour. He felt disorientated, unable to come to terms with what had happened to him, and the meeting with Charlie Spate had unsettled him even further: he continued to go over every word the man had said, seeking nuances, guessing at motives, unwilling to accept the conversation at face value. In the dark night hours he questioned everything he had seen and heard, worried that he had not picked up an intonation, an innuendo: he could not accept that Spate had literally wanted to relax, have a conversation and a drink with him merely because he felt he had something in common with him. He flayed himself mentally with the agonized thought that Spate knew more than he was admitting, that he was playing Eric on the end of a psychological fishing line, that he was merely waiting for the right moment to reel him in, force him to face the fact of Sandra Vitali's death and his involvement in it.

And all the time there was the sullen pounding in his head, the incipient threat of the clawing at his eyes that the pilocarpine now seemed unable to control because of the overwhelming realization that it was only a matter of time, until they called on him, checked on him, did a DNA matching, and asked him to explain how it was that he had been in the murdered woman's bed shortly before she died.

It was coming; it was inevitable, and he felt unable to react, do anything about it, save himself in any manner.

The warm air that met him when he entered the Northumberland Arms was thick with the smell of humanity and beer: a group of university students was noisily competing in a drinking match, pints of Newcastle Brown lined up in front of them; in the corner a darts tournament was in progress, stocky, beer-bellied gladiators enthusiastically supported by clamorous, sweatshirted men clustered together at the far end of the room. It was the North; it was Newcastle; it was normality. He caught sight of Jackie Parton, half watching the activity. Parton's head came around as Eric entered: he caught his glance and he picked up his beer, made his way across on bowed legs and nodded towards the snug.

"Quieter in there."

Eric followed him. The small room was empty apart from a

white-headed, nodding old man who rose as they entered and made his stooped way out into the street. Eric dropped down into a wooden seat, with his back to the wall. Parton looked at him for a moment without comment, and then walked back to the bar. He returned with a double brandy and a small bottle of soda water. "Looks like you need this, Mr Ward. Seems you've had a rough day—"

"More than one," Eric replied, taking the glass from him thankfully.

"Burnin' too many night candles," Parton suggested.

Eric glanced at him sharply, sudden suspicion gripping him, and then gritted his teeth. He was becoming too sensitive, looking for loaded comments where they did not exist. He felt he was out of control now, falling apart, drifting, helpless: he reached for the soda and added some to the brandy. The alcohol was hot in his throat, the soda leaving an effervescent tang at the roof of his mouth.

"You all right, Mr Ward?"

Jackie Parton's tone was solicitous, his eyes veiled with concern. Eric looked at him. Parton was an ex-jockey who had been a favourite on the banks of the Tyne for the prowess he had shown over his racing years at Newcastle. Tyneside had been his stamping ground: he knew Old Benwell and Scotswood, the West End was open to him because of his sporting background; the pubs and clubs of Walker Gate and Byker, Felling and Shields were second homes to him, where he was welcome, and known and respected. The races he had won and the injuries he had sustained were still the stuff of gossip and legend; the story of the end of his career was also well known and recounted with admiration—the Northern mobs, angry at his success; the suspicion of bribery, of races thrown and not thrown; a bad beating...it had all conspired to finish him on the track, but, paradoxically, endear him to the men and women who lived in the shadowland along the river, among whom he could move with ease, and confidence, and respect. It was why Eric had used him over the years, for the necessary inquiries he had to make. He could trust Parton; they had developed a relationship based on mutual respect. He was useful, and effective, because of the wide range of his contacts.

Eric shook his head. "Yes, I'm all right, Jackie. Things have got a bit on top of me, that's all."

"And the Missus?"

Eric smiled faintly: Anne hated being classified in such a typically Northern manner. "She's fine. She's away at the moment—Singapore. Business conference." She had not rung him since her arrival. It could have been pressure of business, it could have been jet lag. It could have been anger. Or maybe she simply wanted some space for a while. He wondered exactly when Sullivan would have arrived in Singapore, and how they would greet each other.

Jackie Parton scratched his broken nose, hunched forward over his beer. "I hear you're representing Tramline Stevens, Mr Ward," he said in a confidential tone.

Eric nodded. "That's really why I wanted to talk to you."

"Thought it might be." The ex-jockey's battered features, scarred with old troubles, expressed doubt. "He's not good news, is Tramline. Always thinks he's ahead of the game, but he's always ten yards back. Thinks he's sharp as a razor, but his edge was blunted years ago. It was the drugs, mainly: he wasn't a bad lad one time, scallywag, of course, but a canny enough lad. His old mother—God rest her—she thought he was a lovable rogue. But he thought he could get into the big time, started dealing, then got hooked himself. It was all so predictable, but he wouldn't listen to his muckers. And the gambling, well, he had a bit luck at the beginning, but he was always a loser, really..."

"You know anything about the business at Gilsland?"

Parton sniffed, shook his head. "Not a lot. The break-in didn't seem to have netted much, and from what I hear none of the stuff has been shopped around. But though the police are all for nailing Tramline over that, it don't seem to me to be his kind of thing at all. It's not his beat. He's a Tyneside water rat—doesn't like travelling too far into the country."

Carefully, Eric said, "He claims he was set up by Jack Tenby."

Jackie Parton's eyes widened: there was a puffiness about them now that Eric had not noticed before. Age was catching up with them all, he thought sourly: the kind of age when everything hurts. It was happening even to the legendary Jackie Parton.

"Tenby?" Parton's voice was sharpened with surprise. "Why would he bother about small fry like Tramline Stevens?"

Eric shrugged. "Stevens reckons it's a way of getting at him over a gambling debt. Rather than breaking his legs, they want to see him inside—"

"Where other bits of him can get broken without a finger being pointed at Tenby," Parton nodded. "Logical, I suppose. But I don't see the big man—"

"Stevens suggests it's been set up by Tenby's enforcer, of course, rather than Tenby himself."

Jackie Parton shook his head gravely. "Ha...They call Tenby Mad Jack, but that's from the old days when he'd swing a pick handle as good as the next man in a bar-room brawl. Things have changed now: he's got licences for his clubs, and he moves with the big noises in the city. Respectable white shirt-front, arl that sort of thing. Dinner jacket for working clothes, even if nothing's really changed back behind. But that bastard of an enforcer he used to use, Terry Morton, he's the mad bugger if you ask me. He's not just hard...he enjoys it so much, you know what I mean?"

"Used to use?"

"The crack is he's moved off Tenby's patch. But I don't know about that." Jackie Parton was silent for a little while, sipping his beer. "So you want me to ask around, find out what I can about this Gilsland thing?"

"It's not just Gilsland. Stevens is being held at the moment on another charge. It's related to murder."

The ex-jockey's wizened features creased in astonishment. "*Murder?* That's crackers! Tramline Stevens wouldn't have the guts to stiff someone, even when he's high as moonlight on crack! Or 'specially when he's high on crack, for that matter. Who's been telling you that?"

"Detective Chief Inspector Charlie Spate," Eric replied. "You come across him?"

There was a short, pregnant silence. "Naw. Not yet—but I don't doubt I will," Parton said ruefully. "I heard of him already. The crack is that he's a hard man, ex-Met, and not too worried about using his boot if necessary. Maybe that's why he came north—got himself too much of a reputation in the big city. Still, up here he's already gettin' some respect, you might say. But murder? He's out of line there. Who are they trying to stick Tramline with? There's been no wild talk in the street..."

Carefully, Eric said, "Two nights ago Stevens was asked to take a message to an apartment near Jesmond Dene. He was injured there, broken arm. His story is he was surprised by a man who was carrying out someone else, on his shoulders. The apartment was wrecked: clearly, the owner had put up a struggle."

"And?"

"Blood everywhere, but the body was carried out, to be disposed of elsewhere. And Stevens sitting there blubbering with a broken arm, high as a kite. So, conspiracy to murder, accessory to murder; maybe murder itself. They're threatening to throw the book at Stevens unless he comes up with a better story."

"So whose flat was it?"

"Sam Cullen."

"Sam Cullen's got whacked?" Jackie Parton let out a slow whistle. "Hell's flames, that'll cause some scrambling on Tyneside."

"You know about Cullen?"

Parton nodded. "So who doesn't? Smart operator. Kept his own hands clean over the years, but he's well known as a good organizer. Some would say not too imaginative, but he put in his systems, ran his business, prostitution at first, then drugs of recent years. But never been fingered by the polis."

"It seems he's been fingered now."

"But not by Tramline," Jackie Parton insisted, his eyes gleaming. "It's just not his scene; not the muscle. He's stupid enough to get involved at the edge, I suppose, but not out in front. He was never a cavalry man."

"He's stupid enough to refuse to give the name of the dealer who sent him to Cullen's apartment. Says he doesn't really know him...or can't remember who it was."

Parton grunted. "Like we both agree—he's stupid. Or it may be something like misplaced loyalty...or fear. So what do you want me to do on this one, Mr Ward?"

Eric considered the matter for a little while. "If Stevens is telling the truth, we need to find the dealer who gave him this so-called message, And we need to find out what the dealer knew—I mean, was it a warning to Cullen to stay away from the flat? If so, how did the dealer know there was danger? And who was it that shoved Stevens down the stairs and broke his arm? Assuming my client is telling the truth, of course," he added ironically.

Parton nodded. "I get the picture. Like peelin' an onion, right? If I can find the dealer, that's one layer; get him to talk, and that's another. Then maybe we'll find out what exactly's going on, get to the heart of this stinker...Cullen, hey? That's a bummer! Man, that's going to cause trouble along the river! There's some bees will be hummin' around that particular pot, believe me!"

He finished his pint and began to rise. "Okay, Mr Ward, I'll see what's going down. It'll take me a few days, talk to a few people, do some sniffin' around. So I'll get back to you as soon as I can and—"

"There's something else." Eric hadn't intended saying them, but the words came out in a rush. He had no plan of action, he remained dead, stunned into inaction by the inevitability of it all, the creeping nemesis that was approaching him, but the words had come out now, unbidden.

"Yeah?" Jackie Parton slid back into his seat, expectantly.

"Have you heard anything about another killing, a few nights ago, in Fenham?"

Parton nodded slowly. "It's been in the papers. A woman. Neck broken. Treating it as murder, they say."

Eric's mouth was dry. His shoulders were slumped, as though under the weight of his guilt. "Her name was Sandra Vitali. At least, that's the name she was going by. It seems she had other aliases—three passports in different names."

"Busy chick," Parton muttered.

"The night she died she was at a reception in Gosforth. Someone tampered with her car. She got a lift home—the police don't know who that was. A couple of hours later, she was dead. There was...an anonymous phone call..."

Jackie Parton was frowning; his eyes had narrowed as he stared at Eric, aware of a wrong note somewhere, discordant to his ear.

"The police are at a dead end so far," Eric went on hesitantly. "According to Charlie Spate they don't know anything about her; they don't know why she was on Tyneside; and they don't know how she made a living...a good living, it seems, from the quality of her apartment."

Both men were silent for a little while. Eric could hear Parton's steady breathing as he waited; his own seemed ragged, uneven.

"So what is it you want, Mr Ward? Was she a client of yours? Or are you acting for the guy who made the phone call?"

"The name of my client is irrelevant," Eric said quickly. "It's...it's a matter of professional confidence..."

"Course. I recognize that. So you want me to do some digging about this woman...Vitali, you said?"

Eric nodded. He blinked hard, feeling the cat stretch slowly, extend its claws. "I want you to find out anything you can about her: what she was up to on Tyneside, who her friends were, what contacts she had, anything...*anything at all.* You understand?"

If Jackie Parton was surprised by the sudden vehemence in Eric's tone he did not show it.

He stood up slowly. "I'll ask around. If she had business...and three passports...there'll be someone around who knows something about her. I might get lucky. I'll see what I can do."

Eric glared at the depleted brandy and soda. "It's important, Jackie," he said in a dull tone. "It's *urgent.*"

"Why?"

Eric hesitated, his tongue rasping sand in his mouth. "The police know she was at the reception in Gosforth Park Hotel. They have a list of everyone who attended—including a man whose face she slapped. Maybe he's involved in all this, but he's out of the country right now. They'll be getting hold of him when he returns. But the thing is, with that list, they'll be able...they'll be talking to them all, everyone who was there, taking evidence. I need to know, before..."

His voice tailed away miserably. The confidence was draining from him; he felt exposed, vulnerable, wishing suddenly he had kept all this to himself, wishing he had said nothing to Parton.

The ex-jockey stood looking down at him. "I'll do what I can, Mr Ward," he said quietly.

After Jackie Parton had gone Eric stayed on in the snug. He bought himself another drink, but nursed it for an hour. He felt reluctant to move, unwilling to face the dark street outside. He felt as though the world was closing in on him, and he was powerless to hold it back. He had changed; his life was suddenly different. Anne was halfway across the world, accompanied by another man. And he was facing a catastrophe, whose dimensions he could only barely comprehend, or was unwilling to accept.

At last he finished his drink and rose to his feet. His Toyota—he still could not bring himself to use the Jaguar—was parked near the Quayside, so he retraced his steps through the Old Market, down the hill towards Amen Comer and back down Dog Leap Stairs. He calmed somewhat as he walked, looked about him, breathing in the past. He liked the old names and the old feel of the place...the Swing Bridge built on the site of the Roman Pons Aelius, named in honour of the Emperor Hadrian; the Sandhill with its timber-framed, five-storied buildings and echoes of an eighteenth-century Lord Chancellor; the chares with their narrow alleys and steps up the steep banks to the commercial heart of the medieval city. Anne could not understand it, but he loved working here from his grubby little office, among the Victorian shipping offices that clustered along the Quayside, memorials of the old, vigorous maritime trade that had made Tyneside a hugely important commercial centre for coal and shipping. All gone now, redevelopment, the new Law Courts, a scattering of restaurants and clubs, a floating nightclub moored on the Gateshead bank...the city had changed. The river had changed.

And the architecture of his own life was crumbling, too.

He was on the Quayside. He could see his car. He slowed his step. There was someone standing near the Toyota. It was Jackie Parton.

Eric walked quietly towards him. Parton was half turned away, staring down towards the black waters of the Tyne as they rippled their way to the sea. Eric stopped a few feet away. Jackie Parton turned: the river mist had lifted somewhat but his face was shadowed and Eric could not make out his features clearly.

"There's something wrong," Parton said.

Eric made no reply.

"I thought I had your confidence, Mr Ward. But that story...you want my help...but there's something you're not telling me."

Eric's tongue seemed to cleave to the roof of his mouth. The slow pounding surge in his temples began to grow louder, presaging pain and anxiety.

"I need to know," Parton said, almost sadly. "This Sandra Vitali. Was it your client who made the phone call?"

There was a long silence, then Eric shook his head. "No. There is no client. It was I who made the call."

"*Why?*"

Eric breathed deeply, the cold air entering his lungs like a knife. "I was...shaken. I...I had an attack, needles in my eyes, panic...I don't know why the hell I acted like that. It was stupid, I should have gone straight to the police—"

"You were at the reception," Jackie Parton said dully. "The police will get around to interviewing you in due course."

"That's right," Eric agreed harshly. "That's why it's urgent."

"Because when they do...?"

"Because when they do, they'll be able to prove that I was with that woman, that it was I who picked her up after the reception, drove her home. They'll have the forensic evidence; they'll be able to prove she was in my car, that I was in her apartment. And they'll be able to prove that I slept with Sandra Vitali shortly before she was murdered."

The words seemed to hang in the air between them. Jackie Parton stood rigidly, making no more sound than a spider.

"They'll be able to fix me with opportunity..." Eric went on desperately, "and probably even suggest a motive, I don't know. It'll all be circumstantial, but it'll finish me. My career, my marriage...so I need to know about her, Jackie. *I need to know.*"

The silence grew around them like a cold fog. Jackie Parton was stiff, his face still shadowed, inscrutable. At last he said in a quiet tone, "I've known you a long time, Mr Ward. We've been involved over the years, and I've always respected you because you was straight. You had a good life, and a good marriage, but I admired you for what you stuck to—you seemed to believe in what you were doing. You had my regard. But this...this Vitali thing is different. What the hell's been going on? What's this all about? You been screwing around. You're involved in *murder.* You walk away from it, you make a telephone call...It seems like I don't *know* you any more. Seems like maybe I never knew you." He hesitated. "You was honest, and you was straight, Mr Ward. I knew where I was with you. But now..." He shook his head. "With this...you crossed a line."

After a moment, he turned and began to walk away. His walk slowed, and he looked back at Eric, shaking his head in regret.

"You crossed a line, and I'm not sure I want to be involved any more..."

In a little while, though his steps still echoed along the deserted Quayside, the ex-jockey's little frame had disappeared in the wraithing mists curling up from the dark sluggish river, and Eric was alone.

3

Detective Constable Elaine Start looked different in jeans and sweatshirt and Charlie Spate was pleased with the transformation. She had a good bosom and he'd been right about her legs. Furthermore, the backside encased in the tight jeans was also worth inspection, he concluded. However, he was here on business and while he could surreptitiously admire the goods, he had no intention of touching them. That had all been in the past, and he wasn't about to jeopardize his new situation with a bit of ill-advised slap and tickle with a junior officer. Even if he was living alone these days, and a long way from his former haunts.

The disco was dark, loud and noisy and the music that boomed out was a repetitious thudding that seemed to hold little of creativity about it. But Spate guessed this was what the younger elements wanted: as for himself, he was long past that phase. He picked up a drink at the bar and when he returned he caught Elaine Start staring at him with a hint of amusement in her eyes. She was jigging lightly in time with the thudding, and he suspected that she could guess what he was thinking.

"Not your style, sir?"

He scowled at her, waved his drink and nodded his head. "You can say that again. Come on, there's only so much of this I can take. Let's get on with it."

He led the way, holding his whisky glass high and threading his way past gyrating dancers, bare shoulders, flying hair and mindless muscle towards the door at the far end of the room. There was a man standing there, dinner-jacketed, incongruous, the bulging of his shoulders announcing he was there to prevent trouble, or to make it for those who wanted to make it themselves.

Charlie grinned at him. "My name's Spate," he announced, "and I don't think you're going to raise any questions about my going through that door."

The big bouncer seemed to be inclined to, but thought better of it. He glanced at Elaine Start.

"She's with me," Spate said, and winked. "Back-up."

The bouncer stood aside reluctantly, and opened the door. There was a short corridor beyond, and then another door covered in green baize. Charlie Spate smiled. These places were all the same. They called it tradition. He described it as lack of imagination.

The room beyond was wreathed in cigarette smoke, and there was little noise. The clamour of the disco was completely shut off.

The clacking of roulette wheels could be heard occasionally, and the low, mannered tones of female croupiers—there was the feeling that attractive, young, slim-fingered women with suitable décolletage could attract more business than male croupiers—but the men who sat around the various card tables were serious, committed, not out merely to enjoy themselves. This was the business of dreams. They held cards expressionlessly; they watched the swift hands of the dealers; they were immersed in private worlds of untold riches, unachievable successes, distant objectives glittering with dull hope. They had the eyes of day and night drinkers, but their obsession was the tables. Spate walked among them, with Elaine Start in tow; he watched, looked at faces, listened and waited.

The monotonous chanting of the croupiers was that of priests in half-empty churches; Charlie Spate looked around. There would be some system of monitoring this whole operation, of course. He soon picked up the security cameras, strategically placed to check all sections of the room. He and his companion were probably already being watched, their entry duly noted. There'd be an office up there somewhere: and the cameras would scan the whole room. It was always necessary in order to keep one eye on the punters and another on the staff. Big money could change hands, and it was not unknown for swift-fingered card dealers to try to bring the house down for their own benefit. Card sharps and card flat...the game was always being played.

"Mr Spate?"

The polite man who touched Charlie's arm was small, slight, dinner-jacketed, and well-groomed. He was smiling deferentially. "Would you be wishing to take a hand? The house could oblige, of course, with some financial assistance, if desired."

Nothing changed, whether it was the Smoke or Tyneside. They were always seeking an edge, always hoping to make a purchase. Spate looked at Elaine Start and grinned. "You want to play?"

"I don't play games," she announced, looking at him levelly, and he knew there was more than one message in the statement.

That was a pity. Spate grimaced. "Me neither."

"In that case," the smooth-voiced man suggested, "perhaps you'd like to follow me and come upstairs? You are expected."

They followed as he threaded his way past the tables until they came to a door at the far end of the room: beyond was a short, expensively carpeted staircase. At the top of the stairs their escort gave a light, discreet tap on the door and then held it wide for them to enter.

The room served as an office and a retreat. It was windowless, to Spate's surprise. Along one wall was the bank of monitors he had expected, which were capable of homing in on any of the tables and effectively gave a complete view of the whole of the gaming room. There were two desks in front of the monitors, with two shirtsleeved men in attendance, staring at the screens. They did not turn their heads as Spate entered.

The man they had come to see was seated on a comfortable settee at the other end of the room: there were easy chairs there, a table scattered with papers, a drinks cabinet. He rose to greet them. He was tall, at ease in his shirtsleeves, sinewy-armed. He was broad in the chest, with short-cropped, grey hair and a craggy, lived-in face. His head seemed to jut from his shoulders like crumbling stone. At some time his nose had been rearranged violently, and his skin was lumpy and tanned. There was something almost reptilian about his eyes, Spate thought: a coldness, a calculation that suggested he always weighed up the odds; but his smile was warm, friendly, and insincerely welcoming.

"Mr Spate."

"And you'll be Mad Jack Tenby."

"Only my old friends call me that. When *you* call me that, *smile,*" Tenby said.

"*The Virginian,*" Peggy Start said quietly.

Tenby turned to her, grinning, one bushy eyebrow raised. "I didn't care for the television series, but I liked the old Forties film."

"Gary Cooper and Brian Donlevy," she replied. "I liked the book. Owen Wister."

Tenby pointed an approving finger at her, clicked his tongue twice, then blew down an imaginary pistol barrel. "And you are…?"

"Detective Constable Elaine Start."

"A film buff copper, at last," Tenby said with a broad grin.

Charlie Spate felt out of things. Roughly, he said, "So this is where you watch all your clients getting ripped off."

Tenby took no apparent offence. "They come of their own free choice. I'm licensed. Inspected. And I run clean games."

"Bit different from the old days."

"We were all young once, Mr Spate," Tenby replied easily. "And most of us grow up. I see you're drinking…can I offer you something rather better?" He turned to the drinks cabinet. "Laphroaig? Glenmorangie?"

Slowly, Spate finished his whisky and nodded, held out his glass. "I'll try the first one you mentioned."

"Miss Start?"

She shook her head and smiled provocatively. "In this company I need to keep my wits about me."

Spate shot an irritated glance in her direction: he got the impression there was some game being played by these two. And Tenby was old enough to be her father.

"So, you're impressed by our set-up here, Mr Spate?" Tenby asked.

"Plenty of punters in the disco," Spate agreed. "And the characters in your casino seem sufficiently intense. And loaded."

A laugh rumbled in Tenby's chest. He rubbed a horny finger along the side of his nose. "Gambling. It's something I never got into personally: always stayed the right side of the fence. Set up the tables but never indulged myself. As they say, the bookie's always the only winner, in the end."

"And *you* are a winner?"

Tenby regarded Spate soberly for a moment, then turned and poured himself a glass of whisky after handing one to Spate. "I reckon so. I've outlived the old days along the river, as you'll have heard, Mr Spate. I've been a wild one. But I've seen the error of my ways, you might say. Now, I'm a businessman. I'm completely legit. I make sure everything is in order, my licences, my operations, everything. I join the right clubs; I get invited to the right functions. I've come up in the world. Hell, you'll even find my kitchens are clean."

"All at arm's length, then," Spate sneered. "Somebody else uses the pick handle these days."

Tenby did not rise to the bait. "You can check me out, Mr Spate," he said evenly. "But you got to talk to the right people."

"Oh, I have done. And you're right. You got it all in place. You move in different circles now, the right ones. But I never believe what I see on the surface. Leopards don't change spots."

The basilisk eyes never wavered as they stared at Spate. A faint smile touched Tenby's lips. "That's as may be, for leopards," he said quietly. He raised his glass. "Your health, Mr Spate...Miss Start."

He waved them to the easy chairs. Spate glanced back at the two men staring fixedly at the monitors. "Don't worry about them," Tenby assured him dryly. "They're not interested in us. They're not even muscle—they're brains."

Spate sat down, Elaine Start in the other easy chair beside him. Tenby lowered himself onto the settee again: he was at least sixty now, but his movements were still smooth, and he looked fit. Spate had heard he worked out in the gym every day without fail. Still a hard man. Whatever circles he moved in.

"So, you asked to come up here. What can I do for you?" Tenby asked.

"Tell me about Tramline Stevens," Spate said.

Tenby shook his head slowly. "Can't say I know the gentleman."

"He's got a real problem: two addictions. He's a mainliner and he's a gambler."

"Sad."

"He owes you a lot of money."

"I'm a businessman, not an accountant. I don't keep an eye on individual gamblers and I don't personally collect the debts owed to me."

"Not like the old days, then," Spate said cheerfully. "But that more or less agrees with what Stevens is saying. There are ways of getting your money, or sending a message, without getting your own hands dirty."

"I'm not sure I quite understand what you're talking about."

"Tramline Stevens reckons you set him up, fixed him to take the heat on a burglary out at Gilsland, so he'd get put inside, where some of your acquaintances could do the necessary with him."

Tenby sipped his whisky with a calm, faintly interested air. "Fanciful."

"So it's nothing to do with you?"

"I've never heard of the man," Tenby said innocently, and smiled winningly at Elaine Start.

"But you've heard of Sam Cullen," Spate snapped, irritated.

There was a short silence. Tenby let out a small, easy whistle. "Ah, now then, that's a different matter. Sam Cullen...yes, I've heard of that...*gentleman.*"

"Tell me what you've heard," Spate suggested. "After all, I'm new around here."

"But not uninformed, I imagine," Tenby smiled coldly. "You'll know as much about Cullen as I do. You know, I never liked the man. He was always out for the fast buck, like we all are I suppose. But there was never any honesty in him."

"I thought there was always honesty among thieves," Spate cut in.

Tenby smiled but his eyes were blue water, turning to ice. "I'm not certain what you're implying, but yes, that's generally what I mean. The old phrase used to have some meaning: we didn't mess with each other in the business. Of course, all that's way behind me now, but I would be foolish to deny that I didn't have my own day..." He winked at Elaine Start. She smiled faintly.

"And Cullen?"

"Like I said earlier, some people never grow up. I got to see the error of my ways. Cullen never did. And there are certain things I wouldn't touch. As a young man, I was involved in the clubs, I did some strong-arming, I had my fingers in a number of pies. I freely admit that, off the record, of course. But never the dirty stuff. I stayed out of the pimping business; I ran no prostitutes; and I never did drugs."

"Mr Clean, hey?" Spate sneered.

"Something like that. Depends on your point of view…your perspective." Tenby hesitated, sipped his drink with thoughtful pleasure. "Cullen, of course, was a hard young man…and you've got to remember there's as much as twenty years and maybe more between us. He ran the streets in the West End, came through the usual apprenticeship—stealing cars, a bit of breaking and entering, the odd mugging of a punter—but he's no fool and he soon climbed out of the mud. Quicker than I did, really," he mused.

"I'm told he had organizational flair."

"Had?" Tenby glanced at him with an air of faint surprise. "Still has, I'd reckon. But it's common talk along the river that he never had the scruples I did—"

"Or that you adopted."

"If you wish, Mr Spate. I'm not talking out of turn here because you already know the score on Cullen, even if you haven't managed to lay your hands on him yet. It's common enough talk he's into the nasty stuff, the kind of thing I wouldn't touch. He's known to run a network along the river."

"So why did you feel it necessary to have him whacked?" Spate asked almost casually.

There was a short silence. Tenby finished his drink, then rose and poured himself another. Spate thought he detected a slight tremor in the man's hand. He refused a top-up of his own glass and remained silent as Tenby sat down again. "Now who's saying Sam Cullen's been whacked?" Tenby asked.

"I am. His flat was turned over. Blood everywhere. But don't tell me you don't already know all this. He put up quite a battle before your enforcer put his lights out. And we got a witness."

Tenby's features expressed only a mild interest. "Indeed. And who might that be?"

"The aforesaid Tramline Stevens."

Tenby smiled sourly. "An addict and a gambler. Hardly reliable. You ever heard the word hallucination?"

"Well, we're putting it together like this at the moment," Spate said easily. "You claim to be legit, but like I said, leopards don't change spots. You must have seen how Cullen's operation has been growing. Was it because you wanted a slice of it? Or was he getting too big, crowding you somewhat? Or maybe there's some other reason we haven't come up with yet. He cross you in some way? Anyway, the word was out that you wanted him removed. Someone tried to warn Cullen but was too late. Your enforcer got there first—but had more trouble than he'd expected. And he had to bundle our witness down the stairs. Even stamped on his arm. Nasty temper. I never met your enforcer…Morton is his name? Sounds harmless enough. But I hear he can lose his cool from time to time."

Tenby was silent for a little while. Then he shrugged. "I understand you have to come around here and hassle me somewhat, Mr Spate. I expect that, even though I've been going straight for some years. It's par for the course. But I assure you, you're sniffing at the wrong tree if you think I've ever been interested in what Sam Cullen's been up to. I don't like the man; I don't have anything to do with the man. And as for whacking him, you can forget it. Not my style."

"Used to be."

"It's the way we were, Mr Spate, long ago and far away."

"I saw *those* films too," Peggy Start murmured. Tenby smiled encouragingly at her.

"So you're saying my witness has got it all wrong. You didn't put your enforcer onto this job?"

Tenby injected patience into his tone, as though he was speaking to a child. "I'll say it again, Mr Spate. I don't know anything about this Cullen business. And you keep using the word enforcer. All right, I'll accept that I gave house room to Terry Morton for some years. I knew his dad, you know, back in the old days. But whereas the old man had control, I'm afraid Terry Morton never did. He never quite appreciated that there were ways of doing things without…violence."

"Like the way you're setting up Tramline Stevens over the Gilsland break-in?"

"I'll ignore that—I've told you, I know nothing about this man Stevens. And as for Terry Morton, my so-called enforcer, we parted company some time ago. I found I no longer required his services. I haven't seen him or heard of him in weeks."

"On his holidays, is he?"

"He no longer works for me, Mr Spate," Tenby repeated levelly.

Charlie Spate nodded sagely, and inspected the glass of whisky in his hand. "Tang of the sea lochs in this, Mr Tenby. But not enough to cover the smell of the bullshit you're giving me."

Tenby gave a slight, dismissive shrug. "Don't look in my direction, Mr Spate. If Cullen's been killed as you say, I'm not surprised—he was always an untrustworthy, slippery bastard. A good organizer but that's all. And you might start by asking where he got his start-up money from. Where'd he get his financial backing? Not from me, that's for sure. No, you're on a wrong track coming to me, I assure you."

Charlie Spate rose to his feet, finishing the Laphroaig. He set the glass down on the drinks cabinet. "Thanks for the drink, Mr Tenby. I'm sure we'll be seeing more of each other."

"Any time," Tenby smiled. "But don't feel you have to rush away. If you'd like some house chips..."

"We'll have a look around, maybe." Spate nodded, and then turned to leave. Elaine Start followed him.

They moved around the tables in the casino for a little while: no one paid any attention to them. Spate knew he'd pick up nothing; he just wanted to irritate Tenby. Finally, they moved back into the disco. The music continued to thud: Spate wondered if it was the same thing they'd heard when they came in. He looked at Elaine Start. "You want to dance?"

Her look was expressive. He headed for the door.

Outside, she shivered slightly as they got into the car. "Well, that didn't get us very far," she suggested.

"Maybe not," Spate replied, starting the engine. "But that bastard knows more than he's telling us. He didn't move a muscle when I told him Cullen's been murdered. I'll bet my bottom dollar he's involved...though quite where Stevens fits in I'm not certain yet. By the way, how are we getting on with the Vitali killing?"

"They've got about halfway through the interviews," she replied as they moved off from the kerb. "They're doing it alphabetically, and they've got a trace out on the guy she belted at the reception. But no one is admitting so far that they knew her. We don't know who she was with, or who invited her."

"Was she a gatecrasher, you think?"

"That I doubt. Someone at the reception knew her, invited her. And we know someone fixed her car so she'd need a lift home."

Spate was silent for a little while. "That guy Ward, Tramline Stevens's lawyer. You come across him much?"

"Not really. He was on the force before my time." She shrugged. "He's got the reputation of being straight."

"He was at the reception. When I had a drink with him, I got the impression he wasn't very happy at the thought of being interviewed about the business. Maybe we should have a chat with him sooner rather than later."

Detective Constable Start sighed. "Don't try to break their routine, sir. Believe me, the guys up here like to start from A and go to Z without sidetracking. They'll get around to Ward in due course."

Spate grunted. "Like they never got around to Mad Jack Tenby. So what did you think of him, hey?"

"I thought he was...rather sweet."

"*What?*" He knew she was winding him up, but he could not prevent the irritation rising in his chest. He drummed his hands on the steering wheel. "And who the hell is this guy Owen Wister, anyway?" he demanded resentfully.

Elaine Start cocked an eyebrow at him. "A Western writer. Friend of Theodore Roosevelt. And grandson of Fanny Kemble."

Irritated, without quite knowing why, Spate snapped, "And who the hell was she when she was at home?"

Detective Constable Start shook her head mournfully, rolled her eyes heavenward, and sighed.

Chapter four

1

As Eric emerged from the magistrates court, DCI Spate was waiting for him in the corridor. Eric nodded briefly, hesitated, then headed for the stairs; Charlie Spate was not to be ignored, however, and fell into step beside him, cheerfully. "You didn't really expect to get bail for Stevens did you? We were bound to oppose it."

"On the grounds he's a suspected serial killer?" Eric asked sarcastically.

"On the grounds that we still want to talk to him, and that he's still not telling us everything he knows. Sweating it out a bit longer might make him change his mind."

"There's nothing in his record that suggests he could have killed Sam Cullen," Eric said evenly. "Or even be involved in the killing. He's strictly small time."

"I'll go with you on that, in general. But he was involved, wasn't he? I mean, he was there. And, there's always an occasion when an opportunity arises to move into the big time, and maybe that's what happened to your client."

"I don't believe that."

At the top of the short flight of stairs, Spate touched his arm. "You got a moment?"

Eric stopped, shrugged warily.

Spate eyed him for a moment, considering. "I thought you'd like to know I been to see Mad Jack Tenby."

"And?"

"He says he doesn't even know Stevens. And, of course, that he never got Sam Cullen whacked."

"Do you believe him?"

Charlie Spate grinned. "I never believe lizards like him, even if they *have* clawed up out of the jungle into the fresh air. But then, I don't believe your client, either. I just thought you'd want to know Tenby is calling it all nonsense."

"He would, wouldn't he?"

Spate chuckled in wry amusement. "Of course. Anyway..." He fished in his pocket, brought out a small folder. "I'm not out to give your client any assistance to get off the hook in any way, but if he says Tenby was involved in Cullen's murder, the dirty deed was likely to have been done by one of Tenby's soldiers. You been around Tyneside a long time—you ever seen this character?"

Spate extracted a black-and-white photograph from the folder. He handed it to Eric. There was a long silence as Eric stared at the features of the man in the photograph. It was an official police file shot: the man stared sullenly at the camera. He had fair hair cut short, a square jaw, cold eyes. His nose was prominent, his mouth set grimly. Eric touched dry lips with his tongue. "Who is he?"

"His name's Terry Morton." Spate stared sourly at the photograph in Eric's hands. "Not a pretty sight, is he? Stevens claims he's Tenby's enforcer. Tenby reckons that though he used to work for him, Morton's not been around for a while. I just wondered whether you'd ever come across him. Whether you might know about his usual haunts..."

The pulse was beating quickly in Eric's temple: he was aware of the thudding, and he wondered desperately whether Spate was aware of it too. "I...I never came across him when I was on the beat," he said.

"Or since?" Spate queried.

Eric shook his head. "No. I've not come across him. Sorry I can't help."

Spate shrugged, retrieved the photograph and put it back into his pocket. "It was a long shot. I just wondered, that's all...I think Tenby's lying, but if he isn't, we still need to talk to Morton, in view of Stevens's claim. Got to look at all possibilities, hey? Keep an open mind. But it looks like Morton's gone to earth somewhere.

Anyway…talking of possibilities, have the lads got around to talking to you yet? About the reception at Gosforth Park?"

Eric felt cold. He shook his head. "Not yet."

"A pleasure to be anticipated, then," Spate grinned and nodded. "Well, keep your nose clean, Mr Ward."

He walked away. Eric turned and made his way down the steps to the street. He was trembling slightly, panic touching his mouth: he wiped it away with a nervous gesture of his hand. He took a deep breath, calming himself. The dull rumble of the traffic came to him, growing in intensity; he stood on the pavement, uncertain what to do, questioning whether he should go back, have it all out now with Charlie Spate. Because he had lied to the man. He *had* seen Terry Morton, just once. It had been a brief, hurried glimpse, but he was certain the man he had seen was Terry Morton.

He was the man who had been coming out of the apartment building, the night Sandra Vitali had died.

But how could Eric tell Spate that, when he had not yet admitted that he himself had been there that night? He gritted his teeth, cursing: he was getting himself deeper and deeper into this mire. He knew what he should do—face up to it with Spate. But it could mean the end of everything, his reputation, his professional career, and he had no proof of his innocence, the circumstantial evidence would point only in his direction.

He was adrift, unable to think straight. And even Jackie Parton was unwilling to help…

It was a quiet, well-behaved area north of Jesmond Dene. The streets were respectable, the hedges well-manicured, the lawns carefully trimmed, the houses solid, expensive, and bland in their smug middle-class superiority. The residents had paid for their own protection with security cameras perched high on the walls, and none of them had been vandalized. Owners of small businesses in town lived here; retired gentlewomen of means and younger widows with monolithic, synthetic bosoms; a few doctors, a dentist or two, a few young lawyers. Not Jackie Parton's kind of area, a world away from the West End and Scotswood, and it made him feel a little uneasy as he sat in his battered car and waited. But the trail had brought him here, so here he was.

He'd asked around about the Gilsland burglary, and there was certainly a feeling on the street that what Stevens was saying might well be true. It was a way of dealing with an irrecoverable debt, because most people believed Tramline Stevens would never raise that kind of money, other than by gambling, but since he was a poor gambler who'd been convinced otherwise by one lucky streak, even that was an unlikely contingency. As for the killing of Sam Cullen, there was plenty of chatter about that, and plenty of theories. Most of them agreed on one thing: Cullen's business had been thrown into disarray by the killing and it wouldn't be long before some kind of war broke out. Though one or two people had hinted there was already a new player on the scene, who seemed to know Cullen's set-up pretty well, and was busy settling it down already.

Mad Jack Tenby could be kicking aside his much-avowed scruples.

As for the dealers, they were mostly a sorry bunch. There were several who he'd already spoken to—they admitted to dealing with Tramline Stevens, but insisted they knew nothing about any message to Cullen the night he had died, and swore they had not been involved. So far, Jackie Parton had found nothing to support Stevens's story.

But the trail led here. Finally, a couple of people had given him a name, and an address. And an hour ago a young man had turned up at the address, gone inside. Parton waited patiently, as dusk began to gather about the neatly ordered streets, and the lights came on, flickering to amber at first, and then to a stronger, whiter light that illuminated the dark corners of the hedges.

The car—a smart Citroën—was parked just outside the gate of the big white house. Jackie Parton yawned. This was a clear distance from the usual haunts of the low-life dealers.

He heard a door slam beyond the gate. He opened the door of his car and stepped out. As the young man in the grey windcheater closed the gate behind him Jackie was strolling down the street. He drew near as his quarry used his electronic key to open the doors of the Citroen; then as the man got into the driving seat Jackie was level, and it was easy to open the passenger door, slide into the seat, and grin at the driver.

"Hi!"

The young man stared at him, alarmed, his narrow, serious face showing hints of panic. He had clear eyes, but his voice was shaky. "Who the hell are you?"

"Nemesis," Jackie said *sotto voce.*

"Get out of my car." The man's voice was uncertain, his tone scarred with doubt. He grabbed a mobile phone, lifted it. "If you don't get out at once I'll—"

"You'll what, sonny? Call the police?" Jackie turned his head, glanced back at the sober, white-painted house with its immaculate flowerbeds. "What it is to have an aged mother, hey? Do *you* pay the gardener? Bet there's no mortgage on that house either, is there? Your mother always lived there?"

There was a short silence. The young man's face was ashen; the pallor was almost fluorescent under the street lights. He swallowed nervously. "I…I've got no money—"

"Don't make me laugh! You been making a packet this last few years. And investing it well, looks like!"

The young man stared at him for a moment, then looked around, peering through the windscreen as though checking to see whether the intruder was alone. "Now look here—"

"Tony, isn't it? Tony Bingham?"

"How do you know my name?"

Parton smiled sourly. "Come off it. You don't think you can deal on the street and still keep your anonymity, do you? Hell, you're dealing with loose-mouthed people, who'll sell anyone for the price of another fix. You're in dreamland, sonny, if you think your name isn't all around the manor."

Bingham was too shaken to deny the dealing. Instead, he asked shakily, "Who are you? What do you want?"

Parton shrugged. "Information, that's all. But this set-up you got here—your mother, I gather. Lookin' after her, is that it?"

Bingham hesitated, then nodded. "She…she's a widow. She's

crippled. Wheelchair-bound." He took a deep breath, gritted his teeth. "I was responsible…"

"Car accident I hear. Negligence. But you look after her well, like a good, middle-class boy should."

"What do you *want*?" Bingham hissed.

Jackie Parton stared at him. He was about twenty-five, he guessed, slim, nervous, agitated. He had quick, intelligent eyes but they were scared now. A high pale forehead, receding hair, the kind of person you'd expect to see in a white coat, hunched over a microscope, in some obscure laboratory. Maybe that's what he'd been heading for, before he went for the main chance. And an easy life, where there was plenty of money to be made, and an opportunity to look after his mother. Tony Bingham loved his mother. And sold shit on the street.

"Talk to me about Tramline Stevens," Jackie said quietly.

There were the usual expected denials, but Jackie was patient. They argued for a while, until Jackie pointed out the obvious. All he had to do was give a name to the police and Bingham's business would fold, There'd be no more big money going into the house he kept for his mother; there'd be the scandal; there'd be a prison sentence waiting for him. And all Jackie wanted was a little information.

At last, Bingham nodded miserably. "All right, it was me. I didn't know what to do. Stevens wasn't one of my regulars I—don't think he even knows my name. But he was desperate, I heard he had no money and needed a fix, so I thought he could do it. He could…I didn't…I couldn't do it myself. I didn't want to get involved, didn't want to get in too deeply. But I felt I had to do *something*…So I used Stevens as a runner."

"To take a message."

Bingham nodded, shakily.

"Was it Sam Cullen who recruited you in the first place? Was he your supplier?"

Bingham nodded. "He gave me the chance. I felt I owed it to him. To warn him."

Jackie Parton stared in disbelief. There was no loyalty among dealers on the street, they were out for themselves, they'd rat on each other to save themselves, but this young idiot clearly felt an obligation towards the man who'd helped him into a stake in the dirtiest business along the river. Tony Bingham was way out of his depth, and didn't realize it. Parton shook his head, almost uncomprehendingly. "All right, you gave Tramline Stevens a message. To warn Sam Cullen. About what?"

Bingham almost whimpered the words. "There was a contract out, to kill him. I tried to warn Cullen. But it seems I was too late." He banged his hands on the steering wheel in sudden frustration. "Look, I don't want to talk about this. Let me go: I've nothing more to say to you. That's all I know."

Parton looked at him curiously. "Now Cullen's dead, has anyone else tried to recruit you, to keep your supplies coming?"

Bingham ran a nervous hand over his mouth, and shook his head. "No. And...I don't think I want to know. There's got to be other ways...I can't keep this up..."

Parton was silent for a while. "All right, I've got one piece of information I needed. Tramline Stevens has been telling the truth."

"He's talking to the police? My God—"

"What the hell do you expect, sonny? He hasn't given your name, because he doesn't know it. But it's just a matter of time, my friend. So you'd better help me, and yourself, right now. You're deep in the clarty, bonny lad, so you'd better come clean and tell me—how did you know Cullen was going to get whacked? How did you get the information in the first place?"

There was a long silence. Tony Bingham laid his head against the steering wheel. He was badly frightened. It wasn't just the exposure to his mother he feared: the knowledge that he was at the fringe of a murder enquiry, his personal vulnerability, his failure to realize the consequences of his actions in getting involved in drug dealing, they all mounted to face him with the horrifying prospect of a jail sentence, or worse. He began to shake, and suddenly the words poured out of him.

"There were three of us. We were at Sunderland University, in the engineering department. The three musketeers, they called us. We were close, muckers, you know? But we were bored with the work, and when we had problems in the second year we all three dropped out. Those bloody lecturers didn't know the real world. We did. We decided to do our own thing, set up our own company. Computer software..." He sighed, shook his head. "It went fine for a while. But none of us were real businessmen. We had cashflow problems. So we had to diversify. Me and...me and Bobo, we'd known the drug scene at university, so it wasn't too difficult to break in. But Bobo wasn't really cut out for it, and he moved south a year or so ago, made a start at a software house again. He's doing OK. But I kept dealing. It was good money, and there was my mother..."

"You said there was a third musketeer," Parton said quietly, when the silence lengthened around them.

Bingham twisted nervously in his seat. "He was always hot on electronics, was Ollie. Electronics, and mathematics. And he was always mad on boats. So he started a sideline of his own when we closed down the software company. He managed to make a few contacts and soon started getting contract work."

"Doing what?"

"Installing electronic gear on boats. You know, the big yachts along the river, and down at Teesside."

"So?" Parton queried, puzzled.

Tony Bingham licked his lips, and stared dully ahead of him, through the windscreen. "Ollie always was a bit wild, with his ideas. It was he who got us started with the software business, really. But he always wanted to push boundaries back. He had big ideas. And the electronics...the gear was mainly for echo-sounding, deep-sea fishing, radiocommunications, hell, I don't really know what it was all about, but it seems he was a whizz with it all, and he got more work, and that's when he decided..."

"Decided what?"

Bingham sighed. "I thought he was crazy. I told him it was stupid. But he had this idea...he thought if he could eavesdrop on some of the rich people who owned these boats, he'd be able to pick up all sorts of information. Stuff like stock markets, business deals, who was screwing whom...he thought he'd be able to use that sort of stuff." He gave a short barking laugh. "I just thought he was bloody nosy, prurient...I never thought he'd get anything he could ever use. But he was convinced..."

"What exactly did he do?"

"He started installing bugs on the boats. I tell you, he's an electronics whizz—"

"Bugs?" Parton exclaimed in disbelief.

"That's right. In the main cabins, usually. State-of-the-art stuff, he reckons. And then, when he went back to continue the work—some of the contracts he had took him six, eight weeks to complete, these boats were pretty expensive, needed sophisticated systems..." Bingham shook his head. "When he went back, he'd collect the tapes, listen to them. Played some of them to me. He had some funny stuff on those tapes." He glanced fearfully at his interrogator. "But then there was one in particular..."

"He played you a tape," Jackie Parton said slowly, "that mentioned Sam Cullen's name."

Tony Bingham nodded quickly. "That's why Ollie brought it to me. He knew I was working for Cullen. He played me the tape. It mentioned there was a contract out on Cullen. We talked about it. Ollie didn't want to have anything to do with it. It scared the hell out of me. I didn't know what to do. I didn't want to get involved, but I owed Cullen, and if this tape was serious, if he was murdered, I'd be on the outside again, and anyway, I couldn't let this happen! I mean, I couldn't just stand on one side and ignore the fact that someone was planning to kill Sam Cullen! But I didn't dare go to him, warn him! I'd have to explain, and I'd get too deeply drawn in, and what if the guys who wanted Cullen dead found out about me, and Ollie, and the bugs? Can't you see? There was nothing else I could do!"

"I want the tape. Has Ollie got it?"

Bingham turned scared eyes in Jackie's direction. "We destroyed it."

"What the hell for?" Parton demanded angrily.

"We didn't wanted to get *involved* in this shit!" Bingham yelped. "I tell you, man, we were crazy there! This was way out, a different league—hell, these people were talking murder!"

"The voices on the tape," Parton asked, gritting his teeth, containing his temper. "You recognize them?"

"How would we know the voices?"

"Were there any names mentioned?"

Tony Bingham shook his head. "No, not really. Apart from Cullen's that is. And somebody called Terry."

Terry Morton. Jackie Parton thought furiously. "This Ollie character…is he still working on the boats?"

"Generally, yes. But not on this particular one."

"Why not?"

Bingham's eyes were round. "Come on! You think he'd want to go back there after he heard that tape? He didn't want any part of it, and neither did I! He was shaking, man. I didn't even tell him that I'd tried to send a warning to Cullen. That would really have freaked Ollie out! We didn't want to be involved!"

Jackie Parton stared at the terrified young man. "If he hasn't gone back to work on that boat, his electronic gear—"

"Still there." Bingham nodded. "He was really pissed off about that. Didn't want to lose it, expensive stuff. But wild horses weren't going to drag him back."

Jackie Parton nodded slowly. "So if the gear is still there, there's a chance there'll be recordings there also…"

Bingham nodded. "Don't know what would be on them, of course." He thought for a while. "But maybe there'll be something about that girl…"

Parton stared at him. "What girl?"

Bingham shook his head impatiently. "Well, I don't know…But I seem to remember…it wasn't just Sam Cullen who was mentioned on the tape. Neither I nor Ollie paid much attention to that bit—after we heard Cullen's name we sort of froze, concentrated on that, played it over…and then, later, got rid of it. But there was another name mentioned. A woman. But like I said, we didn't pay too much attention. But it was something about a donkey."

Jackie Parton stared at him rigidly. "A mule, you mean?"

Bingham struck his own forehead with the flat of his hand. "Yeah, that's right, stupid of me—"

Jackie Parton sat motionless, frozen. Something was making the hairs at the back of his neck prickle. "This…this woman," he asked grimly. "You remember her name?"

Tony Bingham stared at him with round, frightened eyes.

2

From the grassy bank on the steep-sided hill that sloped down to the river they had a clear view of the sea'oing yacht. It was moored in a security-conscious area: chainlink fencing ran around the perimeter of the yard, while at ten-metre intervals concrete posts supported vicious strands of barbed wire above the fencing. As far as they could see there were no guard dogs, although a warning sign proclaimed their presence. The open area of the yard inside the fence held two other boats, which were being subjected to maintenance and repair: the *Lady Ghislaine* was the only craft in the water.

She was painted in white: her sleek, expensive length had clearly been designed for speed, the raking stem and moulded hull marked with a chine line sweeping up to the bow. The boat was at least eighty-five feet in length with an elevated pilot house and a narrow bathing platform aft, protected by stainless steel rails; the aft cockpit was covered with a canvas awning, adjacent to the stern mooring facilities, and steps on either side led up to the main cockpit, the side decks enclosed by half-height bulwarks. The elevated pilot house had been designed to free up the main deck accommodation: down there would be the main staterooms, crew accommodation, and the galley, probably up in the bows. Eric handed the binoculars to Jackie Parton as they sat quietly in the car on the bluff. "I wonder how many crew they'd be likely to carry?"

"Maybe four. That's my guess," Parton grunted. "But there's no one aboard at the moment, that's for sure, so there's no intention of going to sea in the immediate future. As for the yard itself, it looks as though there's only one security guard on duty, in that hut across to the left…"

Eric nodded, and glanced skywards. The light was fading: as the darkness grew about them, leaving a rim of pale pink cloud out at sea, the lights were coming on along the river, gleaming and twinkling in the dusk. In an hour or so, they'd be able to go down to the boatyard, and the mooring.

Eric took a deep breath. He had been edgy ever since Jackie Parton had brought him the news. His mind was in a whirl, as he tried to match up the issues that now stared him in the face: it was a jumble of Tramline Stevens, Cullen, Sandra Vitali and Charlie Spate. There were so many questions hammering at him, scurrying around in his head like agitated rats hunted by a terrier, he was unable to rationalize, bring order to the chaos, fix his mind so that he could bring some logic to bear. But now, anxiety and excitement coursed through his veins. When Jackie had met him in the bar at the George and Dragon and given him the information he'd received from Tony Bingham, Eric had grabbed the little man by the shoulder, turned him so that he could see his features more clearly.

"Sandra Vitali! Her name was mentioned on the tape?"

Almost sullenly, Jackie Parton shrugged his hand away. "It seems so, Mr Ward." As he took a pull at his beer, there was an air of irritation about the man: it was clear to Eric that the ex-jockey was not entirely happy with the turn of events. He still had a chip on his shoulder about Eric's behaviour; he had been reluctant to get involved in the Vitali situation, but now it had been forced upon him by the information he had obtained from Tony Bingham.

"And the tape's been destroyed?"

"Seems so. And Bingham can't remember what was said...he only vaguely remembered her name, after I prodded him a bit."

"What about his friend?" Eric asked urgently. "The one who planted the listening device in the first place?"

"Ollie. He's seen the error of his ways," Parton replied sourly. "I went to talk to him. But friend Ollie has disappeared. He doesn't want to be involved. He's got sense, that lad. Late in the day, but he's got sense, not wanting to get involved in this mess."

Eric was aware of the implied criticism. He brushed it aside. "So what do you make of it all?" he demanded.

Jackie Parton's features rarely expressed surprise and only occasionally doubt. But his voice betrayed his uncertainty. "It would seem there's a clear link between Sam Cullen and Sandra Vitali. I think she worked for him. You told me that DCI Spate informed you the dead woman had three passports. On the tape, it seems she was referred to as a mule. That means one thing only as far as I'm concerned: Sam Cullen has been running a drug supply operation on Tyneside, and she's been involved in bringing the stuff into the country, probably from South-East Asia." He sighed, shook his head in despair. "It's common enough for the gangs to use young women—they recruit gullible youngsters from Manchester, Liverpool...they meet them in the clubs, promise them a free holiday in an exotic location, all expenses paid, often with sex added as a bait, and then when it's time for the girls to return they're given packages to carry, or their bags are broken into and drugs planted, in the expectation that the mule won't get picked up at the airport. It's common, and it's widespread, and though there are a few stupid young women rotting in Bangkok jails, most of them actually do get through."

"And Sandra Vitali?"

Parton grimaced. "A bit different. Not like the usual, stupid, gullible, but generally innocent, mules. Clearly, she was in deeper, involved more often, employed in the organization. My guess is she'll have been travelling with, or for, Cullen, maybe on a regular basis, though sometimes using different identities. She was close to him, I reckon, important..."

Eric nodded, feeling cold realization sweep through his veins. She had told him, the night she died, that she'd got in deeper than she'd expected. She wanted out, and she was scared... "So if she was linked with Cullen, if her name was mentioned when his murder was being planned, it's obvious that there's a link between the two killings."

"I would say so," Parton agreed.

Eric realized he now had something to say to Charlie Spate;

there was information he could give, which would draw attention away from his own involvement with Sandra Vitali. But it would still be at a price—he would have to admit to having picked her up, been in her flat, made love to her, and every instinct drove him to wait, stay uninvolved in the inquiry, cross the bridge of his own guilt only when he was forced to. There was another consideration: the information Jackie Parton had obtained could not be confirmed: the word of a drug dealer, and a tape that had been destroyed. It wasn't enough.

"If this man Ollie has left his equipment on the yacht, there's the possibility it will have picked up other information," Eric suggested.

It had already occurred to Jackie Parton. "That's my guess," he shrugged.

"The listening device…it could contain information about who killed Cullen, or who was given the task. Cullen…and Sandra Vitali. Jackie, you've got to help me. I've got to get on that boat, recover the equipment that's there. It could supply me with the answers I need."

Jackie Parton stared hard at him for a long time, and then sighed. But old loyalties overcame his more recent prejudices. "I was afraid you were going to say that."

They left the car on the hill; and made their way down to the road below, scrambling down the bank, slipping and sliding under cover of darkness. The road was unlit, but a bright light glowed in the security guard's hut at the far end of the boatyard. They moved quietly along the length of the chainlink fencing. Eric kept a close lookout: Jackie Parton had already told him, disapprovingly, that he had crossed a line: now he was really diving into murky waters. Breaking and entering: it wasn't exactly a suitable occupation for a lawyer and an ex-policeman. But he didn't feel he had any choice.

They reached the padlocked gates. "What do we do now?" Eric whispered.

Jackie Parton ignored him. It was clear that this was no new experience for him. Eric could not see what he was doing, but the ex-jockey had produced some kind of implement from the pocket of his dark windcheater and he was twisting and turning it in the padlock, swearing lightly to himself as he did so.

Eric glanced towards the security hut. He thought he could make out the form of a man inside, standing with his burly back to the window. Eric looked up above them: there was a glimpse of windblown stars, the moon was rising but it was partly cloaked by scurrying clouds, and a sharp breeze had now sprung up, whispering secretively along the river. Beyond the gleaming outline of the *Lady Ghislaine* he caught sight of the dark rippling waters of the Tyne, slapping lightly against the hull.

There was a light click, and a sigh of satisfaction from Jackie Parton. Gently he eased the padlock out and carefully hung it on the chainlink fencing. He opened the gate slightly and looked at Eric. His face was expressionless but in the faint moonglow his eyes were gleaming, excitement from an adrenalin surge he could not subdue. "Last chance, Mr Ward, last chance to walk away from this."

Eric shook his head. "We've come too far," he muttered.

They stepped inside the gate and looked towards the security hut. They could just see the top of the guard's head through the window: he was seated; it was likely he was reading. Jackie gestured towards Eric and they slipped across the darkness of the yard, as long faint moonshadows picked out the cobbled surface of the quay. Under the hull, the boat was bigger than Eric realized: the superstructure towered above them, as they moved quietly aft, hidden now from the window of the security hut. Jackie glanced back at Eric and then reached out, gripped the rail and lightly climbed the ladder to the aft deck: Eric followed him. A transom window lay in front of them on the aft deck: probably the window of the master cabin. Both men had taken the precaution to wear rubber-soled shoes: now their progress was almost soundless as they crouched low on the aft deck and made their way towards the steps leading up to the pilot house.

There was a pause, the light rattle of skeleton keys in Parton's hands. The wait seemed endless: the moon drifted from behind the clouds and gleamed on the polished railings of the yacht.

Somewhere in the distance, across the river, he heard a group of men singing drunkenly: Eric peered over the side and made out the lights of a pub on the far bank. Jackie Parton wrestled with the locked door, and then straightened. "All right," he whispered tensely, "we're in."

The pilot house was dominated by a dash that expanded across and below the front window, housing instruments and electronics. Air conditioned, it was additionally ventilated with side windows and an aft door. The helm position was separated from a small social area by a counter top extending from the port side, with an adjacent bar. The pencil light of Jackie's torch glittered briefly and longingly on the gleaming bottles, and then flickered away, dancing along the walls, halting finally on the sliding hatch that led to the cabins located on the lower deck. Jackie whispered hoarsely to Eric. "It'll be somewhere down there, according to Bingham. In the main stateroom."

They climbed down the steps into the lower deck passageway. The crew quarters would be at the bow, the guest cabins lying between the engine room and the crew. They moved cautiously along the passageway: the saloon was positioned aft, past a small dining area and leading to a main entrance hall on the starboard side. Jackie flashed his torch about: the hall was linked to the upper and lower decks with a single flight of stairs. They eased their way through the small vestibule, past the airlock doors into the master suite.

By the light of the torch they were able to pick out the soft yellow leather of the chairs and settees, the cherrywood panelling, the table top finished in burl wood. They were safe here as far as lights were concerned, out of the line of sight of the security hut. Heavy curtains had been drawn across the cabin windows: Jackie twitched them aside carefully, peered out and nodded in satisfaction. "We're overlooking the far shore. The guard won't pick us up here, even if he looks out of his hut." He flashed the torch beam around the cabin, at the drinks cabinet, the refrigerator, the pull-out cocktail preparation shelf, the audio-visual entertainment centre. There was a shower room attached: its walls and floor were sheathed in Verde Rajasthan marble. Jackie Parton whistled appreciatively. "Pack of money gone into this..."

Eric wasn't interested. He was edgy, nervous: he wanted to get the job done quickly, so they could get out of this situation. "Did Bingham give you any idea where the bug might have been placed?"

"Not really," Jackie replied softly. He began to move around the cabin, touching, peering, checking. Eric produced his own torch, bigger, a stronger beam. He was careful to keep it low, avoiding the curtained portholes, aware of the presence of the guard on the dock. The combined light of the torches reflected enough illumination to allow them to cover the cabin twice, going over the same area, checking on each other's progress. Eric was sweating profusely in the close darkness; Jackie Parton was making small sounds of irritation, frustration.

"Are you sure Bingham said his friend had planted the device in the main cabin?" Eric asked.

"He said he thought it was. Near a chart. It would be the obvious place, for the kind of information the damned kid was hoping to get," Jackie snapped. "But—" He stopped suddenly, the pencil beam wavering, then fixing on the bulkhead, the framed chart located just to the left of the small alcove. He moved forward, reaching out, felt gingerly behind the frame, in the small narrow space at the back. Then he turned his head, grinned at Eric. "I think—"

Next moment they both froze. There was a light tapping sound against the hull, and then a scrambling noise, the sound of heavy boots on the deck. "*Bloody hell!*" Jackie whispered.

"What is it?"

"The security guard."

They stood still, rigid in the darkness, their torches clicked off, the darkness thick and heavy about them as they listened to the slow pacing on the deck above their heads. Jackie had closed the door behind them: now they heard the rattle of keys, and they knew the man would be checking the interior. They crouched down, away from the windows, and waited. Blood was surging through Eric's veins, pounding in his head as they waited: the movements above them, on the bridge, were casual enough, indeterminate; it was as though the man was wandering, looking over the controls. After a few minutes all fell silent: they heard the soft creaking swing of a leather chair, and then the faint odour of cigarette smoke.

Eric glared in the darkness in Jackie Parton's direction. They were trapped below: there was the other method of egress, up the stairs in the small hallway aft, but they did not dare try it for the noise they might make, attempting a locked door. The guard was in the pilot house, swinging in his seat behind the wheel, enjoying a cigarette, perhaps dreaming dreams of Caribbean nights he would never experience, warm Asian waters he would never see, the lights of far distant ports...

"You think he suspects anything?" Jackie whispered.

Eric shook his head. "I don't think he's heard or seen anything. This will be just a routine check: breaking the boredom of the night watch. He's relaxed, smoking..."

There was the slithering sound of Jackie Parton seating himself. "Then he could be a while. We might as well get comfortable too."

Eric was too tense. His ears strained for the slightest sound, but all he could hear was the slow, swinging creak from the bridge as the guard smoked, and looked out over the river from the bridge, and dreamed his dreams. It seemed an age before boots finally clattered on the deck again, and the man began to move. But it was no occasion for relaxation: his steps came towards the companionway that led down to the main cabin.

Jackie lightly tapped Eric's arm, then his fingers gripped Eric's forearm, drawing him forward silently, gently. "Move quietly," he hissed. "Back towards the sleeping quarters. Down towards the head."

They slipped through the darkness on their rubber-soled shoes. The guard's heavier, measured tread echoed on the companionway as they eased themselves along the corridor, towards the head. There would be an escape route there, Eric guessed, but to take it would mean noise, alerting the guard. Parton stopped, pressed Eric's chest, pushing him back against the wall, squeezing himself into the blackness under the rear companionway.

Reflected light glimmered and flashed in the main cabin. The guard was peering in, checking, using his flashlight, flickering the beam around the walls. But he stayed on the companionway; he made no attempt to enter the cabin. After a short while the light faded, and they heard him returning to the bridge. Eric let out his breath with a long, shuddering sigh. They waited in the darkness, unmoving. The steps wandered again about the bridge for a little while, and then the silence came back. Some minutes later, while they remained frozen below, they caught the sound of the door slamming. The guard had left the bridge: he was dropping back down to the dock. He began to whistle, a plaintive, mournful, erratic tune as he clumped his way back towards the security hut.

"I dreamed I dwelt in marble halls," Parton muttered.

"So?"

"It means bad luck, whistling that."

"For us, or for him?" Eric asked.

"I hope to God he doesn't check the gate," Parton hissed. "If he does..."

Eric didn't want to think about it. He waited, listening, his nerves on edge. There was no further sound from the cobbled dock. He breathed a sigh of relief, and glanced at his companion. "Did you find anything back in the cabin?"

Jackie Parton flicked on his pencil beam. In his hand something small gleamed dully. "He'd fixed it...a tiny microphone...behind that chart. There's a built-in tape, tiny, but it was placed to pick up any sounds, any conversation in the main cabin. Made in Japan. Clever little bastards, those Japanese. There's even a playback device, I think..."

"We'd better get out of here," Eric said fervently.

"Not for a while," Parton suggested. "Give that guard time to settle down."

"You think he'll be relieved at some time? That could cause a problem for us."

"I doubt it. This'll just be a night shift. And his coming aboard, I think it was just curiosity. He didn't see anything."

Eric hoped Parton was right. He leaned against the bulkhead, his eyes becoming accustomed to the darkness again, now that Jackie had switched off his torch. There was still the faint odour of the cigarette the security guard had enjoyed. "I could do with a fag myself," the ex-jockey grumbled. "Gave them up a year ago, but right at this moment..."

They waited in the darkness. Eric had noted a small door at the entrance of the master suite; now, curiously, he opened it and peered inside. He guessed from the weight of the door that it was soundproofed, the room beyond clearly designed for confidential business. In common with so many modern yachts, he realized, the *Lady Ghislaine* had been equipped with a small study opening onto the stateroom. The room itself was small, narrow, bookcase-lined, well-equipped: a satellite-based video link, tiny red and green lights gleaming at him steadily in the darkness, a modem, a printer, a fax machine, a scanner. The cabin was fitted out as a soundproofed, secure, confidential office.

"Jackie...Tony Bingham had no idea who owned this boat, is that right?"

"His friend Ollie just said it was a big company. Not from around here. He thought it was registered down south. As for whose company, or who was speaking on the tape, he just didn't know. And he didn't think Ollie knew either."

But with an office on board, there might be some intimation, some answers...Eric entered the cabin, flicked on his torch, shone it around at the bookshelf in the comer, the twin desks, the computer with its attachments. He sat down on the swivel chair at the desk, fumbled for the switch and turned on the computer. The screen glowed greenly at him; he tapped the keyboard, entering the system as it clicked and flashed at him. Moments later he was into the main files. He trundled through them: they were meaningless, most of them seeming to refer to matters relating to the boat itself. But there was a correspondence folder. He tried to open it. It demanded a password, but when he cancelled it he was still allowed entry to a small group of files. He knew he'd not get into anything really important, without a password, but he decided to check them anyway.

He looked through the files. Something flashed up. It was a copy of an insurance document, for the *Lady Ghislaine.* Eric peered at it. The owner was named as EMF Enterprises Ltd. The registered number was also noted. It meant that Eric could do a search at Companies House and discover who the owners were. Possibly. He suspected it would not be as easy as that. Companies registered at Companies House would usually provide the minimum of information, and would shield the reality of ownership behind nominees, individuals or other companies, sometimes registered offshore. But it was a start.

He tried the Internet options, but was barred from email messages by the need for a password. He trawled through the remaining files but found nothing of interest. After a while, he stopped. He could bear some kind of static, behind him. He turned his head, listening. A moment later, Jackie Parton slipped into the cabin. "I been trying the playback," the ex-jockey whispered. "I think young Ollie isn't the whizz-kid he made himself out to be. There's a problem…Any case, it's best to check it ashore. And I think it's time we made a move."

Eric nodded agreement. He turned back to the computer, scrolled through the files again, but could see nothing that might be of interest. He closed down the system, clicked off the main power, and then there were only the red and green lights, steady, unwinking. He flashed the torchlight around the cabin once more as he rose from his seat, ready to move out, following his companion. Then he paused. The beam of the torch settled on the fax machine. An edge of white paper gleamed in the light. Eric leaned over. There was no message waiting to be read: it had already been removed. But in the careless tearing of the sheet from the fax, a fragment of the paper had become detached and part of a line had been left. It contained a series of numbers. They began with a zero, followed by a one and a seven. Eric frowned, thinking, then carefully teased the section of fax paper from the machine. He slipped the fragment of paper into his pocket.

They left the boat silently, creeping over the deck, dark shadows against the waxing moonlight. Jackie Parton locked the door behind him, and they slipped down the companionway aft, down to the cobbles of the boatyard. The light from the window of the security hut gleamed steadily: they could see the guard more clearly now. He had his feet on the table in front of him: he was reading his paperback again, one arm thrown behind his head.

The padlock still hung on the chain fence. They moved silently into the roadway, and Parton clicked the padlock back into place. He took a deep breath, relieved that the tension was over. They climbed the hill again, got into the car, Jackie Parton behind the steering wheel.

"Try that tape again," Eric suggested.

Parton nodded, and took the device from his pocket. It was little larger than a matchbox. He peered at it, pressed something. The static hissed at them. They sat, listening, but could make out nothing. Jackie Parton cursed. "If you ask me I think we've been on a bloody wild-goose chase, boarding that damned boat. We've got nothing for our pains." He glared at the box in his hand. "Still, I'll go see a guy I know, find out if it's possible to get any enhancement of this, but it sounds to me like our friend Ollie is nowhere near the electronic wizard he's been cracked up to be. Either that, or there's been no more conversations on that bloody boat."

Eric felt deflated. "Let's get away from here," he said flatly. There was a weariness in his body, the adrenalin washing away, disappointment taking its place. He was left in a greater dilemma than ever, he thought, as Jackie started the engine, pulled the car away towards the main road, away from the bluff. To his earlier fall from grace, he could now add breaking and entering.

Below them, they caught a last glimpse of the *Lady Ghislaine*, long, elegant, shimmering pale against the dark waters of the river.

They drove back towards Newcastle, silent, each immersed in his own thoughts. After a while Eric remembered the scrap of torn fax paper in his pocket: he fished it out, smoothed it.

He looked at it in the faint gleam of light in the car. Then he fumbled for his torch, switched it on, inspected the line of figures.

It was a fax number, he guessed: the number of the office which had sent a fax to the *Lady Ghislaine.* It could be from the company that owned the vessel. He stared at the figures and something moved dully, foggily, in his brain. It looked as though there were perhaps two numbers missing at the end of the sequence. They would, of course, be crucial in identifying the sender. But the rest of the numbers, up to those last two, were somehow familiar to him.

He felt cold, and angry suddenly.

They were numbers which he had used himself, in his own office, from time to time. He didn't have the last two digits on this scrap, but he could guess what they were.

3

The phone dragged him from a drugged sleep.

Eric turned over in bed and looked at the clock: it was four in the morning. After the tension and excitement of the break-in on the *Lady Ghislaine* he had tumbled into bed at the flat in Gosforth, exhausted. His mind was a whirl, a turmoil of questions and wild theories, but surprisingly, in spite of the activity in his mind sleep had come quickly. But it was a heavy, dragging experience, and as he woke now he was mentally sluggish. It took him several seconds to realize it was Anne's voice on the phone.

"Where are you?" he asked, stupidly.

"Are you all right?" she asked.

"Half asleep, that's all. It's four in the morning."

"Oh, hell, sorry, I didn't think. I'd just been to the office and…well, I'm sorry I've not rung before, but we've been very busy, and Jason has been wonderful! We've managed to button up the details of the licences, remarkably quickly, so we should be coming home this week, sooner than expected."

All that seemed to register with him was that Jason had been wonderful. He shook his head, clearing his senses. "I'm sorry...You're coming home this week?"

There was a short silence. "You don't seem particularly excited about the prospect."

"Aah, really, I'm sorry, I'm just not really awake, you know? So the business is completed?"

"Things went remarkably smoothly. The guy they brought in from Malaysia was remarkably efficient, quite charming, and clearly is a man of some influence. He cleared all the logjams in double-quick time, he's related to the Minister so the timber licences were arranged just with a couple of phone calls, Jason was on hand to tie up the legal loose ends and the whole thing's virtually done and dusted. There are contracts to be signed, of course, but Rashid has assured us that everything now is just plain sailing."

"That sounds great."

There must have been a certain coolness in his tone. It affected hers. "Yes, well...what about your end of things?"

"My end of things?"

Impatience edged her voice. "Yes. Have you sorted out that takeover for Shoreline Investments?"

Eric cleared his throat. "More or less. Leonard has been playing silly buggers again, of course, and has twisted the cord around the throats of the Barker people. I'm not entirely happy with the way he's going about things—"

"So what's new?" she interrupted briskly.

Eric hesitated. "Anyway, it looks as though we should sort things out today: there's a final meeting to agree terms. But he's really screwed them down—"

"And you clearly don't approve. Well, Eric, you and Leonard never did see eye to eye, did you? However, as I said earlier, we'll be flying back this week. And it so happens that Rashid—that's the man who's smoothed paths for us out here in Singapore is coming to England at the weekend, on a business trip. I've invited him to get over his jet lag up at Sedleigh Hall, with us. I think it would be a good idea to invite Leonard also, for the sake of form, and Hallam, since we're representing him in the Barker Marine takeover. I can get all the details then, and it'll also be useful perhaps to undertake a certain cultivation of Rashid—he could do things for us in our Asian venture. Will you let them know up at Sedleigh, and get the arrangements in hand?"

"I suppose so," he replied grudgingly.

"You sound odd."

"I'm all right. A bit…disorientated, that's all."

"I rang Sedleigh. They told me you haven't been back since I left. Have you been so busy then, in Newcastle?"

"Things…have been happening," he said lamely. For a moment he was seized by a wild urge to tell her everything that had occurred, his stupidity, his anxieties, the break-in on the *Lady Ghislaine*, but the words died in his throat. Betrayal was a harsh word. Maybe he could still sort all this out without Anne ever knowing about it. It was pointless worrying her now, with so much still unresolved.

"Will you be asking Jason Sullivan to Sedleigh?" he asked.

There was a short, pregnant silence. "Naturally," she replied in a calm tone. "Eric, when I get back, maybe after the weekend, I think we need to talk…"

"Yes," he replied dully. "I think we do."

What was scheduled to be the final meeting between Barker Marine and Shoreline Investments was to be held in Joe Hallam's office, in the tower block near Gallowgate.

Eric arrived early and stood alone in the resplendent conference room with its long, gleaming table, precisely arranged desk pads, shining decanters of water already arrayed for the small group who would be dealing with the final arrangements. Eric had a sheaf of papers he would need to circulate: the Barkers would obviously want to instruct their own lawyers on the detail but if the purchase price could now be determined, and the conditions met, it was all over bar the shouting.

Not that there would be much of that, he thought drily; he had gained the impression that the fight had gone out of the father and son team. The presumed loss of the defence contract had undermined their confidence: his guess would be that they would now cave in, and accede to whatever deal was offered them.

He stared out towards the Town Moor, past the tall gantries of the Gallowgate football field lighting system, and thought about Anne's call. He wondered what she had meant, when she had said they needed to talk...The way they had been when she left for Singapore, the intervening silence, and now the early return with Jason Sullivan in tow...It added up to something he did not want to contemplate. But there were other things he was reluctant to think about also—Sandra Vitali, Charlie Spate, and last night's crazy escapade with Jackie Parton. His world had turned upside down: he had prided himself all these years on his independence, his sticking to ethical principles, his walking of a straight line where there was no room for compromise. And now, over a matter of mere days, it had all been blown sky high. He could hardly come to terms with the manner in which his life had changed, and was changing...and he dreaded what he was going to have to face in the future. Both the immediate future, and also the longer term, where he would have to live with the consequences of his actions.

Jackie Parton was right: Eric Ward had crossed a line and there was no turning back.

Behind him, the door opened. The young secretary seemed startled when she saw him. "Oh, Mr Ward, I didn't realize you were already here. Is there anything I can get you? A cup of coffee?"

Eric nodded. "That would be most acceptable. Are the others on the way?"

"Mr Channing is with Mr Hallam in his office. The other side...they're in the waiting room. Would you like me to send them in to join you?"

Eric hesitated, then nodded. "Yes, I think so."

They arrived at the same time as the coffee. Fred Barker hobbled in belligerently, still clinging to the hope that he could bludgeon a better deal out of his opponent Joe Hallam. His son Rick was more subdued: he was a realist, Eric guessed, and knew that the hand they held did not contain too much bargaining power.

They were accompanied by a lean, sallow-featured man in a pinstriped suit. He was introduced to Eric as their legal adviser, Mr Paine, from Paine and Stewart.

Eric shook hands, and when they informed him they had already been served with coffee in the waiting room, he invited them to sit down. "The others should be here in a short while, gentlemen, but while I take my coffee perhaps you'd care to look over these papers I have with me. They don't prejudge any issues this morning, but it might be useful if we could get some of the preliminaries out of the way before we get down to the main business." He handed around a sheaf of papers, a bound set for each of the three men. They received them in silence, the lawyer Paine the only one expressing any real interest, leaning over them shortsightedly, almost sniffing at them in his search for legal flaws.

"The first document is the proposed recommended acquisition of Barker Marine," Eric explained, "It includes a summary of the terms and the structure of the transaction. You'll find details of the related break fee, settlement terms, and taxation implications. The second document contains a summary of the key agreements—"

"Including the guarantees we called for?" Fred Barker rasped.

Eric looked at him levelly. "I am under no instructions to include such a clause."

The architecture of the old man's face seemed to crumble somewhat. Nick Barker laid a hand on his arm. "Not now, Dad," he advised softly.

"Then there's a composite deed of indemnity," Eric continued, "summarized financial information, and I've also included a summary of the Barker Marine articles of association, which you'll need to check, to advise me if they are accurate. And finally, the special notices that are required, the special general meeting, the resolutions that will need to be duly passed..."

The sallow-featured lawyer leaned back in his chair, and folded his arms. "I'll need to go through these in more detail, of course," he said in a reedy voice. "But in general, it seems you have covered everything."

He seemed to be about to say more, but Fred Barker interrupted him. "I been in touch with the department in London...the defence people." He glared accusingly at Eric. "I got nothing out of them."

"I warned you, Dad," Nick Barker soothed.

"They'd neither confirm, nor deny what Channing was on about at our last meeting. I heard about you, Mr Ward: you're well enough known on Tyneside. Everyone reckons you're straight. Do you really go along with what's happening here?"

Eric hesitated. He held the man's fierce glance, and slowly shook his head. "You have to realize, Mr Barker, I can't be expected to voice a personal opinion here. I'm representing the interests of Martin and Channing, as financial advisers to Shoreline Investments, and—"

"So you're no different from the rest of the bastards, then," the old man said in dismissive disgust. Eric felt the blood drain from his face. Maybe the old man was right. Maybe, in the course of the last years, more than one line had been crossed.

They sat in silence for the next few minutes: the old man contemptuous, his son staring at his hands, their legal adviser riffling through the documentation provided by Eric. Finally, the door to the boardroom opened and Joe Hallam strode in. He made no apology for keeping them waiting, but took his seat at the head of the conference table, nodding briefly to the small group assembled.

Behind him came Leonard Channing. Eric stared at him coldly, but Channing failed to meet his glance. Suddenly, it seemed to Eric, Leonard Channing was looking his age. His normal suavity seemed ragged; there was a grey pallor about his features, accentuated by two spots of burning colour in his cheeks. His skin had a dry look about it; his lips lacked colour, and Eric thought he detected a slight shake in the man's hands as he drew forward the chair and seated himself. His eyes flicked up briefly to meet Eric's: they seemed lifeless, hooded and slow. Eric stared at him, puzzled—the fire seemed to have gone out of Leonard Channing. Eric wondered whether there had been some kind of argument going on with Hallam, in the confines of the private office at the end of the corridor.

Hallam was staring at Eric, his displeasure evident. "Looks like you started the meeting without us."

"Not really," Eric defended himself. "I've just passed around some papers. It'll save time."

"Not that I expect this to be a long meeting," Hallam barked harshly. He seemed edgy, annoyed, his fingers drumming on the table. "This thing's been going on too long already."

"I'd still like to know—" Fred Barker began belligerently.

"The time for asking questions is over," Hallam interrupted rudely. "There's only one question that's to be answered now. It's a simple one. You already have the terms on which we're prepared to purchase the company. Are you prepared to accept them?"

"The guarantees we asked for—"

"Are you prepared to accept them *unconditionally*?" Hallam bludgeoned.

There was a short silence. The legal adviser to Barker Marine cleared his throat. "I would have wished to know—"

"Who the hell are you?" snapped Hallam.

"My name is Paine, and I'm here as the legal adviser—"

"Lawyers only clutter up business deals," Hallam sneered. "And the time for lawyer talk is over. I'm not prepared to spend any more time on these issues. I want signatures on documents. No more talk. No more questions."

There was a light sheen of sweat on Hallam's forehead. Eric frowned. Something had happened. Hallam had always displayed a brutal, direct approach in his business dealings: negotiations for him were like a bare knuckle contest. But things were different today: it was as though he was out of patience and time. Eric guessed the man was under some pressure himself, and he wondered what it could be. Beside him, Leonard Channing was silent, grey, his glance lowered.

Paine drew himself up, thin-shouldered. "I can hardly advise my clients—"

"Look," Hallam interrupted. "Maybe you haven't heard me

clearly. I've been waiting for months to get clearance on this deal. My shareholders have come to the end of their patience. Barker's is dead in the water, we all know that. There's been too much bluffing going on—too much huffing and puffing. I don't give a damn for your workforce; your defence contract is nothing more than a chimera; there are no other buyers waiting out there, and the price Shoreline Investments are offering is a fair one. But it's no longer negotiable. I want a decision today."

"You don't fool me, Hallam," Fred Barker almost exploded. "You're not about to bully me into signing anything that—"

"No?" Hallam's features were like granite as he stared at the old man with evident dislike. "You been jerking me around too long, Barker. So I'm finished with playing around. You need to know—*I've called in your credit.* Tell him, Channing."

There was a long, tense silence. Leonard Channing raised his head slightly, looked at Barker. He grimaced, twisting his mouth. "Mr Hallam has become…distressed by the dragging out of negotiations. He asked me to talk to the houses that have been financing your business for the last six months. You had had an extended line of credits..." He paused, blinked as a spasm seemed to cross his lean features. "That line of credit was predicated on the belief that you would negotiate a reasonable price with Shoreline Investments. I have spoken to the banks in question: when I told them the realities of the situation, that Mr Hallam will pull out unless papers are signed immediately, they were only too happy to cover their potential losses. Your credit lines have been transferred, gentlemen. And now…"

"It's I hold your paper," Hallam snarled triumphantly. "So let's be clear. I'm not holding off. Either we do the deal today, and have a smooth passage, or else I call in your paper, and you're sunk anyway."

"What the hell do you get out of that?" Fred Barker flashed, his craggy face suffused with anger. "If you close us down—"

"I'm not stupid," Hallam averred. "Calling in your paper will mean liquidation. That's delay. A purchase is still a better option for me: I want to get this shoreline development finished within the next six months. But if you still keep jerking me around, don't get me wrong. I'll close you down, even if it means me taking a loss on the deal. I'll close you down, tomorrow, and I mean it."

He was serious. They all knew it. The silence grew around them. Nick Barker's mouth was set in a grim, defeated line. He knew it was over for the family company he and his father had wanted to save. He stood up, glaring at Hallam. "It seems you're leaving us no choice."

"Damn right!" Hallam agreed sourly.

Fred Barker struggled to his feet, also, standing shoulder to shoulder with his son. "Who's pulling your chain, Hallam?"

The question seemed to infuriate Joe Hallam. His cheeks were livid, his eyes gleaming with barely contained rage. "I want those bloody papers signed by tomorrow afternoon, or else I scuttle your company and see all your precious employees on the street!"

"I don't see how we can do that," Nick Barker argued. "We've got to look at—"

"As far as I'm concerned, you can sign the papers blind. You've got no choice." Hallam stood up, knuckles on the table, shoulders hunched, glowering at them like a prizefighter determined to intimidate his opponent.

Fred Barker seemed to want to say something, but his son touched his arm. Paine gathered up the papers Eric had provided, with a sniff. All three men trooped out of the room without a further word, Rick Barker helping support his half-crippled father. After they had gone there was a short silence. Hallam broke it with a grunt of satisfaction. "Right. That's it. Now then, Channing, you follow through on this. I want those papers signed by tomorrow afternoon. You can fill Ward in with the detailed picture regarding the credit lines. Now I've got other things to do." He began to walk to the door. Halfway there, he stopped, thought for a moment, then turned, looked back at Eric. His voice had changed, mellowed somewhat. "I understand we'll be meeting this weekend."

Eric raised his eyebrows.

"A call came through this morning," Hallam went on. "It's about an invitation to join you and your wife at Sedleigh." He paused; the sheen of sweat was still on his brow, but he seemed calmer now. "I look forward to the occasion." His glance slipped past Eric, to Leonard Charming. "I understand you also will be there, Leonard. Quite a party."

He left the room. The door closed behind him; Eric stared at it thoughtfully. Anne had certainly worked quickly: the invitations had gone out from her office base in Singapore almost as soon as she had contacted him, so she must really regard the dinner party as important.

He turned to Leonard Channing. The chairman of Martin and Channing was still seated. He seemed to be having some difficulty with his breathing. "Are you all right, Leonard?" Eric asked.

Channing nodded, his lips pale. "Well enough. A bit...a bit breathless, that's all. My age, I suppose..."

"You have an argument with Hallam?"

Channing shook his head. "No. It's just that...I don't feel too bright today. Food poisoning, maybe. That lobster, last night..."

Eric hesitated. The man seemed ill, and it might not be the best time to question him, but Eric had to know whether his suspicions were justified. He leaned forward, stared at Channing. "I've had occasion, from time to time, to use your own private fax line—not the one in your office, but the private one, at your flat."

"Yes?" Channing was unable to inject any interest into his tone. He began to rise. "I think I'd better get back to my hotel. I'm a bit shaky, and—"

"I came across a fax number last night," Eric said. "It looked like your number, though the last two digits were missing."

Channing ignored him. He began to walk across the room, his steps somewhat faltering.

"Tell me, Leonard—have you ever sent a fax to the *Lady Ghislaine*?"

Channing had reached the door, he put his hand out, gripped the door handle. "*Lady*..." He seemed puzzled, as though he had only partly heard the question, or had not grasped its point. Then something gleamed in his eyes, deep, secretive, scared. "I...I don't know—"

"Tell me, Leonard," Eric insisted coldly, "what do you know about the *Lady Ghislaine*? Who owns the boat?"

"I don't know what you're talking about," Channing almost gasped.

But he did know; Eric was convinced of it. And other, half-formed questions tumbled in his head. "More to the point," he said slowly, "if you've had dealings with the *Lady Ghislaine*, did you also know Sandra Vitali? You know, the woman who was murdered a few nights ago?" As suspicion grew in his mind his voice hardened. "Was it you she was supposed to meet that night, at the reception at Gosforth Park?"

Channing gave a light moaning sound. There was panic in his eyes. He opened his mouth to issue a denial but the words were strangled, incoherent. He was sweating suddenly and there was a fluorescent pallor about his face. He leaned heavily against the door, sagging, and his eyes were glazed. For a moment, Eric thought it was because of the thrust of the questions he had put to him, but then he realized it had another cause. Channing's fist was up, kneading at his chest. There was a blur of pain in his eyes now. He put out a hand towards Eric, as though seeking support and he lurched, staggering towards the younger man. "Help me..." he moaned in a strangled tone. Startled, Eric put out a reluctant hand.

Next moment the older man was pitching forward, falling towards Eric, knees buckling, eyes rolling upwards. Eric failed to catch him in time. Leonard Channing collapsed, rolling on the carpet. For a moment he twisted, dragging his knees up so he was almost in a foetal position, and then he gave a single convulsive shudder and lay still. Eric leaned over him; Channing was still breathing, but it was a stertorous sound, slow and agonized. Eric stood up, crossed swiftly to the door and flung it open.

"Get an ambulance quickly," he ordered the startled receptionist. "I think Mr Channing's had a heart attack."

Chapter five

1

Charlie Spate stared sourly at Mad Jack Tenby. "This is an unexpected pleasure."

Tenby ran a hand over his craggy features and smiled expansively. "Well, you know the old saying. Mountains and Mahomet. We had one little chat, in my club. I thought now it was about time I came to see you, sort of bearding the lion in the den."

"I would always have been happy to come to see you, Mr Tenby," Spate replied easily. "If I thought you had something to say. Of importance."

"Well, I was in the neighbourhood, you know." Tenby's smile had hardened a little at the edges. "And it's always on the right side I like to be, you know, civic-minded, eager to help the police in their inquiries."

Spate humphed cynically. "That'll be a first, is my guess."

"Not at all, not at all, Mr Spate," Tenby replied, taking no offence, but his eyes were watchful. "There've been occasions when I've been able to pass on certain information to the right quarters. I think you got the wrong idea about me. But then, you're not a local lad. You're new to Tyneside..."

"There's nothing different about Tyneside," Spate suggested.

"Ah, that's where you're wrong," Tenby disagreed. "Up here, we got respect for the law. We don't always follow it, when we're young and excitable, but as we get older, we see the errors of our ways. It's the clean northern air, you see: it gets the blood rushing when you're young, but it brings wisdom as you get older."

"Crap."

"Aye, well," Tenby grinned. "That's as may be." He leaned back in his chair in Spate's office, at ease with himself. "The fact is, bonny lad, I been hearin' things. About me, I mean. There's been talk. I was at a dinner the other evening. There was chat, like. Gossip. Emanatin' from this office, like. So I thought maybe I'd call in to see you, so we can clear up any misunderstandings there might be between us."

"Such as?"

"Such as I'm a respectable businessman, and I don't like nasty rumours circulatin' among my friends."

"Your new friends, I suppose you mean," Charlie Spate sneered.

"Everyone moves on," Tenby replied, his eyes glittering. "Usually upwards. Of course some people like you, well, they just get sidetracked. Or sidelined. Enjoy life up here, do you?"

Spate felt anger stir in him but he controlled it. "So you're getting upset because some of your new county friends are hearing stories about you."

"Untrue stories." Tenby drew his eyebrows together thoughtfully. "You see, it's one thing coming along to my club, talking to me in the privacy of my office, tellin' me straight how you see things." He grinned, wolfishly. "That I can take. But things is different when you start shooting your mouth off elsewhere, causing me problems, embarrassment among my friends. Now, that's not nice. So I thought I'd call in, let you know how I feel. And maybe let you know I've never been a lad who takes things lying down, you know what I mean? You start callin' me, maybe I'll have to do something about it."

"You're not going to *sue* me are you?" Spate asked in mock astonishment.

Tenby's eyes glittered. "Have your little joke. But come on, bonny lad. All I'm saying is don't push it too far. I already told you, I've moved up in the world and I've got new connections. You're fresh around here, but you've brought baggage with you. I've heard about some of the little problems you had back down south. We wouldn't want all that to be stirred up around here, now, would we, Mr Spate?"

Spate stared at him contemptuously. "What's the matter, Tenby? You afraid we're getting too close for comfort?"

"All I'm saying is—"

"You're saying you got big friends, who'll put a word in for you, make life somewhat uncomfortable for me. But my life's always been uncomfortable, and that's a problem for you because I don't give a damn. I know what's been going down, and I'll prove it. I know why Sam Cullen was killed—and pretty soon I'll even know how it was done and who done it, as they say."

Tenby was silent for a little while, watching Spate keenly. "I already told you Terry Morton left me some weeks—"

"And I told you that's all mush! Sam Cullen was running a drugs operation and you wanted in. So you decided there was only one way, and that meant removing Cullen. So you put your pet dog onto him—"

"I told you I don't do drugs—"

"Didn't, you mean," Spate sneered.

Tenby grunted, heaved himself to his feet, no longer at ease, displaying annoyance. "Hell, it's no good talking to fuzz like you. You got a problem, you. It's called stupidity. The hell with it. I've told you how I feel; I told you there's strings I can pull, puppets I can make dance. If you aren't prepared to make sense—"

"So you've heard, then."

There was a short silence. Tenby stared at the policeman, chewing something over in his mind. "Heard what?" he asked suspiciously.

"Heard we found Cullen's body," Spate announced cheerfully. "What else?"

Tenby was breathing hard. He stood there stiffly, ruminating, digesting the information and the likely consequences it might have. It wasn't to his taste. He nodded slowly, glowering at Spate. At last, he said, "So tell me."

"Messy job. Making a point, I suppose, but I always thought you Northern characters was more sophisticated. Yeah, we found the burned-out car, down at an isolated headland south of Marton Rock. Petrol splashed around, burned out completely. Body inside, then the whole caboodle shoved over the edge onto the rocks below." He shook his head admiringly. "You pick your minders well. Was he ever on the lump? There's a building site nearby—so it seems Morton had some skills. Seems as though once he'd whacked Cullen, and stuck the body in the car, and burned it, he used one of the mechanical diggers there, to tumble the wreck over the edge. We're checking those right now. Think we got the one that was used. Neat little man, your Morton, though. I mean, fancy returning the digger, putting it back where he found it! His mam must have brought him up proper. Told him he always had to put back things he'd borrowed. Or maybe it was you taught him well. Keep things neat."

"You're going to try to tie this to me?" Tenby suddenly lost his temper, his lips writhing back in a snarl. "I'm telling you, it would be better if—"

"Fact is, who knows what'll turn up with forensics?" Spate wondered pleasantly. "They got the body right now. Or what remains of it. But let me assure you, Mr Tenby, I'll certainly keep you informed of the progress of the investigation. Since you're so *intimately* concerned…"

Mad Jack Tenby looked for a moment as though he would like to return to the old days: his hands clenched spasmodically, memories of a pick handle still clear in his mind, and his mouth was grim. But he took a deep breath, remembered his new image, controlled himself, and after a moment, he nodded, as though satisfied about something. "All right, Mr Spate. You have your little jokes. But don't step on my toes too hard. You might end up losing a foot."

He turned abruptly and left the office.

Charlie Spate leaned back in his chair with his hands behind his head; he wondered whether the Chief Constable knew that Tenby had decided to visit headquarters. It was just possible, even, that he had suggested it. They belonged to the same clubs, after all, he thought sourly to himself.

He sighed. He was less confident than he had appeared to be in front of Tenby. The report had come in late last night, about the car, and the body. The amazing thing was no one had come forward to say that they had seen the blazing wreck at the coast.

But that was the way of the world, he thought sourly. The lucky thing was that an off-duty copper had been walking the headland and had seen the wreck down below, along an isolated stretch of the coastline. He'd scrambled down to investigate, and there it was.

The charred corpse was with forensic at the pathology labs now, but it would be a few days before they came up with anything. He shook his head. Even Tenby should have known better: torching a corpse couldn't hide everything. There was teeth, for a start. As it happened, the killer had been careless anyway. They'd found a distinctive ring on the body: the chat was that Cullen used to wear a similar ring. So that was all right. Still, the problem was going to be trying to link the killing to Tenby and his organization. The key to that was the enforcer, Terry Morton.

He'd gone to ground, that was clear. Tenby would have ordered him to lie low, make himself scarce for a while. The call was out, of course. Find Terry Morton, and everything would slip into place.

The phone on his desk rang. He picked it up. "Someone to see you, sir."

"Who?"

"The solicitor, Mr Ward."

Charlie Spate groaned mentally. Tramline Stevens again. He shook his head. "All right. Send him up."

Half an hour later Spate sat staring at Eric Ward, his blue eyes all ice and cold light. "What the hell got into you?"

Eric shrugged, made no reply.

"You must have known we'd find out eventually..." He had sat dumbfounded as Eric Ward had told him the story. How he had seen Sandra Vitali at the reception but had not spoken to her. How she had approached him in the car park when her car failed to start. How he had driven her home, then accepted her invitation to go to her flat.

"Are you *really* expecting me to believe you went up there because she said she needed legal advice?" Spate had asked disbelievingly.

In stiff tones, Ward had replied, "It wasn't exactly like that. But does it matter? I admit I went to her flat. As you'll find out, from the prints I left."

"Among other things...whatever it was like, you ended up screwing her," Spate sneered. "And then you walk out of the door, realize you've left your car keys and you go back...and bingo, there she is."

"I had nothing to do with her death."

"So you say. But it was you who covered her up with the dress."

"I...I didn't like to see her...leave her like that."

"Touching. Sensitive. And it was you who made that phone call, anonymously." Spate shook his head in disgust. "You did just about everything wrong, didn't you? What the hell got into you?"

"I was disturbed...I was shaken, and I was in pain. I couldn't think straight. Anyway, I'm here now."

"Bit bloody late! But just before we come to check you out anyway." Charlie Spate brooded for a while, watching the solicitor distrustfully. "All right, now you are here, is there anything else you want to say? You tell me you were with the dead woman that night; that she was killed in the short interval between your leaving and your return...is there anything else?"

Eric Ward nodded. His eyes were uncertain, but he seemed almost relieved to be getting rid of a burden that had been weighing him down. "I saw the man who probably killed her. He was leaving the building, as I came back."

Charlie Spate sighed. He waited. "And?"

"I think it was the man...you showed me a photograph."

"Terry Morton?" Spate leaned forward, his interest quickening. "You say it was *Morton* you saw? Why the hell didn't you tell me this before?"

Eric Ward met his angry glance levelly. "How could I, without admitting I was there in the first place?" He leaned forward, urgently. "Thinking back, I can see how it was planned. Morton must have intended killing her earlier. He'd ripped out the wires in the car; maybe he intended dealing with her in the car park. He must have been waiting there in the darkness. But before he could deal with her, she approached me. I gave her a lift. So he followed us, then waited until I left the building. Then he went up there. He rang the bell. She probably thought it was me, coming back for the keys, or whatever. Maybe she was just fuddled with sleep. But she went to the door. Opened it..."

Silence grew between them, Ward uneasy, nervous.

"How could Terry Morton have known Vitali would be at that reception?" Spate wondered.

"He would have been informed, of course."

Spate thought back to the list of men who had been at the reception. Tenby's name had been among them...he felt the earlier slow crawl of irritation being dampened by a quick exhilaration, realizing he might yet be able to link this to Mad Jack Tenby.

He was not about to give that away to Eric Ward. "What a bloody mess," he growled to himself. He squinted at the man facing him. "All right. So it's conscience brought you here? But why now? Because it was only a matter of time before we questioned you? Before we found out that you'd been with the dead girl anyway, from DNA samples?"

Eric Ward shook his head. "No. It wasn't that. Of course, I was worried about your check. But put yourself in my place. I was shaken, and confused: I'd behaved stupidly by going there in the first place, and then by covering it up afterwards. But there were...things on my mind."

Like your marriage. And the threat to your lifestyle, Spate thought cynically. "I bet."

Spate's tone was discouraging, but Ward ploughed on. "I felt there was so much circumstantial evidence building up against me: forensic would have picked up my DNA, traces might well have been found in the Jaguar when I gave her the lift—I just felt I needed to try to find out more myself. Who she was, to start with. I needed to find out why she died, who killed her—before I admitted anything."

"Because you think coppers are liable to develop mindsets," Spate sneered. "Hell, you ought to know—you been one. The fact is, by not coming forward before now you've slowed everything down. You've made it more difficult—"

"No. I don't see it that way." Eric Ward's head was up, and there was more confidence in his tone.

"You wouldn't!" Spate exploded. "But by coming here, what do you hope to gain now? You've not got off any hook! We can throw the book at you, for obstruction of justice! And we might still just pin the whole thing on you anyway!"

"No," Eric Ward said firmly. "Because you wouldn't be able to tie me in to the killing of Sam Cullen."

Charlie Spate leaned back in his chair, the anger receding; a coldness crept into his veins.

"Why would we want to try to do that anyway?" he asked curiously.

"Because the two killings are linked."

The two men sat staring at each other, holding glances, neither giving way. After a while Spate muttered, "You'll have to explain that to me. We've picked up no connection—"

"Sandra Vitaii worked for Sam Cullen. Or at least, there was a close connection. She was a mule; she took part in smuggling operations. That's why she had the passports you told me about. It looks to me as though someone is trying to break up the drug dealing arrangements under Cullen's wing. Just look at it logically. First, Sandra Vitali gets killed; then, within days Cullen also gets murdered. If Terry Morton killed Vitali, it's likely his next target was Cullen—"

"Why?"

"Because they were *linked*, dammit!"

"We've found Cullen's body," Spate said, almost dreamily.

"It has the hallmark of a gangland dispute," Ward said.

"More than that," Spate muttered. Silence fell between the two men, then Spate opened the drawer of the desk in front of him. He took out a manila folder, and opened it, studied the contents for a little while. "This just came in this morning," he said.

"What is it?"

"Interpol report." He looked up, met Ward's glance. "It seems a man—a British subject known to the police—was killed recently, at the international airport in Malaysia. He was being followed;

there was a tip-off before he left Thailand. The customs authorities lost him in Kuala Lumpur, but picked him up again at KLIA. He would have been arrested when he arrived at Heathrow. But he never even made the plane. Now…it seems his ultimate destination…he was headed for Newcastle. Not the usual runner, it seems—a stand-in. They'd been expecting a woman..."

"Sandra Vitali?"

"Maybe." Spate thought for a little while. "I hadn't put it all together, but maybe it does begin to make some sense. There's a takeover in the offing: it starts with a killing in Malaysia; the next to get whacked is Sandra Vitali, the mule; and then it's the turn of Cullen, the organizer, himself…" He turned an inquisitive glance upon Eric Ward. "But just how did you pick up this link?"

He saw the hesitation, and he knew he would not be getting the entire truth. Eric Ward shook his head. "I still have contacts from the old days. You know how it is…how you can get information from the street. I was put in touch with some dealers…but you don't need to know that—"

"I think I do."

"I do not." Ward's tone was firm. The room was still, tension crackling between the two men. Then Spate decided not to push things, not just yet.

"You got the information from drug dealers? Not exactly reliable witnesses. But still…"

"It didn't come from them directly…" Eric Ward was choosing his words with care. "Let's just say, the information I got led me to another source." He took a deep breath. "I don't know how it all fits together, but I can give you a name."

"A name…" Spate said thoughtfully, wondering what Ward was still holding back.

"The chairman of a merchant bank in London. Leonard Channing."

Spate opened his eyes wide in surprise. "What the hell is that supposed to mean? A merchant banker?"

"I can't prove it," Ward said stubbornly, "but I believe Channing knew Sandra Vitali. My guess is that he had arranged to meet her at the reception in Gosforth Park. In fact he didn't turn up. I would doubt very much whether he was involved in the murder of the woman, but he knows something about her background—and someone would have introduced him to her in the first instance."

Something in his tone puzzled Spate. "Martin and Channing. Isn't that the bank you're involved in, on your wife's behalf?"

"It is," Ward replied stiffly.

"And you don't like this guy Channing."

"That's nothing to do with it. I think he's linked in some way to Vitali. I give you the thought. What you do with it—"

"Is my business. I see. Channing's back in London, I suppose."

"No. He's here in Newcastle." Eric Ward hesitated. "But there's a problem. He's had a heart attack. He's in intensive care."

"*Bloody hell!*" Charlie Spate returned the manila folder to the drawer in disgust.

There was a short silence. "Anyway," Ward said slowly, "in the circumstances, I don't think you have any reason to keep Tramline Stevens in custody any longer."

Charlie Spate glared at him. "Mr Ward, I don't think you're in any position to be asking bloody favours here!"

2

Late winter sunlight dappled the hillside. There was a fresh breeze blowing in from the Cheviot under high, scudding clouds and on the fell a scattering of sheep, early returners from the lower stretches of grazing land, dotted the dark green of the distant slopes. The whistling and yelling of a distant shepherd calling to his dogs came in on the breeze and high in the sky the white stitching of a plane track began to unravel, dispersing into fluffy trails. It was good to be back.

Eric had returned to Sedleigh Hall on Friday afternoon, and late that evening Anne also had returned. Their meeting had been somewhat perfunctory: she was tired and jet-lagged and had decided to sleep in the spare room across the corridor from him. She had told him that their Malaysian guest would be arriving at midday on Saturday—the others, excluding Channing, would be joining them at the hall by late afternoon.

He had told her about Leonard Channing's collapse and explained that he was still in intensive care, in a coma. He had told her about nothing else, though he suspected she was aware that something was wrong. Maybe it was his demeanour; maybe his reticence.

His dilemma was acute: he had now told most of the story to Charlie Spate, the police had conducted an interview with him, they had taken a sample of his hair for DNA testing and he was sure that it would check out with the evidence they had culled from Sandra Vitali, but he was uncertain what information would be released in due course, and its timing. This could be the opportunity to try to explain things to Anne, but he shirked it.

To tell her might mean the end of his marriage; and yet he had the sinking feeling that the situation and the consequences might be worse if he did not tell her now, hoping the truth would never emerge. He was gambling and he knew it.

"All right," Charlie Spate had said to him sourly, "you've come clean, or so you say, and we'll just leave it there for the moment. I'm not going to prefer any charges; we've got other lines of inquiry to follow up, I want to get the forensic report on Cullen's body, we need to check up on Channing and the possible link you claim he had with Vitali, and then I'll certainly want to get back to you. It would have been better if you'd told us all this earlier, but, in the circumstances...well, just don't do anything else stupid, while we review the whole situation...But you'll need to make a written statement. Detective Constable Start will take it."

The news would get out among the inquiry team of course, and after that it would soon become a matter of common gossip within the force: the ex-copper who had turned brief had shown at last that he wasn't the upright, straight character he'd always made himself out to be. There'd be a certain amount of crowing in some quarters, he knew. The taste of it was sour in his mouth, but there was the other matter that bothered him still—he hadn't come clean with Spate, not entirely. Maybe he should have told him about the *Lady Ghislaine*, but that would have meant admitting to breaking and entering. He was in enough trouble as it was. And he did not feel he could tell Anne about any of it.

As for her, something was changed.

She didn't really *appear* any different, although a certain amount of strain was obvious in her eyes. It could have been due to the rigours and effects of a long flight, but he had the feeling she had changed in some subtle way, in the short period she had been away from him. They had had no opportunity to talk much when she arrived home, but she was up and about early—another consequence of jet lag—so they were able to breakfast together in the long, tall-ceilinged room that looked out over the meadow, sloping down to the river.

She wore a light blue, flowing robe emblazoned with a Chinese dragon breathing fire: the sort of thing tourists would buy in the department stores in Singapore. It wasn't her style; he was surprised by it.

"A gift," she explained. He didn't ask her who had bought it for her.

"So the business went well?" he queried.

She nodded enthusiastically. "It really did. We got on rather better than I'd expected. Jason had told me we were likely to be in for a long haul, but once Rashid popped out of the hat everything seemed to go like clockwork. So, the short account of it all is that we've managed to secure the timber concessions from Malaysia, the licences have been agreed, the Californian company has backed off—I think there will be some compensation payable there, but it doesn't affect Morcomb Enterprises, and it's all go! We'll be setting up a new subsidiary in Singapore itself, so that we have local representation, and really everything has gone perfectly." She paused, almost defensively. "It was just as well that Jason was there, because his knowledge of corporate law was essential, and, it seems, they knew about him. He's had dealing with Singaporean officials before..."

"And this Rashid..."

"He's a Dato'—the sort of equivalent of a knighthood in

Malaysia. Very well connected, has his fingers in a number of pies, sits on the board of some very large public companies, and a bit of a go-getter, which can be unusual for ethnic Malays, I believe. He's been instrumental in paving the way for us in Singapore, and he's got burgeoning business interests in the north of England, it seems, so it seemed only sensible to offer him our hospitality."

Eric had difficulty getting out the next words. "He's coming up here this evening…Jason Sullivan?"

"He'll be in about four this afternoon." She was successfully avoiding his eyes, as she sipped her breakfast coffee. "I think we'll have to settle for a fairly late dinner."

Dato' Rashid bin Abdullah proved to be the life of the party. He was of middle height, dark-haired, perhaps forty years of age. His dark skin was clear, his black moustache luxuriant and his brown eyes sparkled as he conversed with wit and charm. He was extremely handsome, Eric thought, and knew it: he told them of his early days in Malaysia when he had displayed entrepreneurial flair by selling second-hand rubber tyres for scrap, and how he had progressed to becoming a successful businessman, being invited to take seats on a number of large mining, timber and computer software companies. He was open enough to stress that some of this activity had been the result of the form of ethnic nepotism developed by a Malay government keen to promote Malays over the Chinese elements in business society, but Eric was still left with the feeling that much of Rashid's success had been due to his own driven personality. And, though he might be charming, apparently easygoing, and witty in his compliments to his hostess, there were occasional hints of the man behind that social facade. Eric guessed there would be steel in Rashid's personality, a ruthlessness that all successful businessmen could display from time to time. The kind that Hallam showed, in a more brutal manner.

Joe Hallam himself was somewhat subdued. He took little part in the conversation, listening to Rashid and chatting quietly to the Lord Lieutenant, who was often a makeweight guest on these occasions: Anne felt that it was useful to invite the Queen's representative in the county to dinners where overseas businessmen were to be present. They tended to be rather impressed by that, although Eric himself was less than impressed: the Lord Lieutenant was a dull dog, a former Brigadier who took himself very seriously. In his contributions to the conversation, pomposity ruled.

"I gather that it was in your office that Leonard Channing collapsed," Anne said, attempting to draw Hallam into the conversation.

"Eric was there," Joe Hallam replied abruptly. "I didn't actually see it. He's still in intensive care..."

"I've met Channing; we're members of the same club," Jason Sullivan commented. "He's got a good reputation in the City...as you'd well know, Eric."

Eric nodded, making no comment, and Sullivan turned back to speak to Dato' Rashid. Eric watched him for a little while. He was clearly on extremely good terms with the Malaysian businessman—that would be the result of the work they had done together in Singapore. They were about the same age, both handsome, well-groomed, with an easy charm. Jason Sullivan, like Rashid, was aware of his good looks—quick smile, keen grey eyes, fair hair that flopped boyishly over his forehead. He had taken silk at an early age, after a successful, meteoric rise in the field of corporate law, and he had acted as a consultant to Morcomb Enterprises for two years now. Anne rated him highly for his professional skills, Eric knew.

But the question that nagged at him was the extent to which she rated him personally.

He had tried to thrust away such thoughts for some time, but he had been aware of the strange light that could appear in Anne's eyes when she spoke of Jason Sullivan QC. The public school accent grated somewhat on Eric, but Anne hardly seemed to notice it. Sullivan was suave, confident and apparently unmarked by the kind of uncertainties that dogged Eric. He played squash regularly, had been awarded a rugby Blue at Cambridge, and counted among his friends some of the most successful lawyers in London. And tonight, he had barely spoken to Anne, while she herself hardly seemed aware of his presence.

It could have been due to the fact that they had spent two weeks together in Singapore and now sought other conversational partners; on the other hand, it could have been caused by something else, here in Anne's home, with her husband sitting opposite her. Eric was aware of a certain tension between Anne and Sullivan, the kind of tension that made them avoid each other's eyes. He was unwilling to question too deeply what might motivate their constrained behaviour.

When dinner was over the group moved into the library where coffee and brandy was served. Eric found himself standing near Hallam, at the fireplace. Hallam glanced at him and nodded. "My first visit to Sedleigh Hall. Impressive."

"My wife's family," Eric explained.

"Well, one of these days, if business continues to go well..." Hallam rumbled. "Did you get the papers signed?"

"The Barkers? Yes, they've put their signatures to the documents."

Hallam eyed him, with a gleam of barely suppressed contempt. "You didn't like the way I handled that, did you?"

Eric shrugged. "It's your business."

"Channing knew what I was after. And he played along with it."

"Leonard was never over-imbued with sentimentality," Eric replied.

There was a short, uncomfortable silence and then Hallam said, "The police been to see you yet?"

Before Eric could reply, he became aware that Anne had drifted across to them. "Police? Now what would they want with my husband?"

Hallam was startled; he glanced uncertainly in Eric's direction, and then he grimaced. "We were both at the businessmen's award dinner. In Newcastle. There was a woman there. It seemed she got murdered, later that night."

"Good God!" Anne exclaimed. "But why would the police be talking to Eric?"

Hallam shrugged. "It's no big deal. It seems they have to

interview everyone who was at the dinner. Routine, I suppose. Cross-checking statements...that sort of thing. I had my session with them few days ago...nothing I could say to help them, of course. I didn't know her, don't know who she was with, or who had invited her. The papers have been calling her a mystery woman...if you'd been here, you'd have heard about it. Been splashed all over. I just wondered whether Eric had been put through the mill yet."

"And have you?" Anne asked, turning her curious glance on him.

"I have," Eric replied, injecting a carelessness into his tone that he did not really feel. "With the same result. I...I told them I didn't know her."

He had never been a good liar, and he was aware that something in his response had alerted Anne: she knew him well and she clearly felt his reply had been somewhat lacking in conviction. She was staring at him in an odd way, reflectively, almost as if she was looking at a stranger, and he felt himself flush. He turned away, glanced uncertainly at Hallam and almost without thinking said, "Do you think maybe Leonard Channing knew her?"

He should not have said it: Anne's scrutiny had unnerved him. Hallam stared at him; something moved, deep in his eyes. He frowned. "Why would you think that?"

"I don't know..." Eric floundered. "I suppose it was just...something he said to you the next day, at the meeting with Barker Marine. He asked you if he'd been missed."

Hallam laughed shortly. "That's hardly enough to link him with a murdered whore."

"Was she?" Anne asked quietly.

"What?" Hallam blustered, uncomfortable under her piercing gaze.

"A whore."

Hallam was at a loss for a moment. He finished his glass of brandy. "I don't really know, of course. But it's what the police suggested to me. I mean, she got killed in her apartment...and I gather there were circumstances that suggest...well...Er...do you mind if I replenish my glass?"

"Of course," she replied coolly. She turned to Eric. "What did the police tell you?"

He shrugged. "Not much. Her neck was broken. She was in her own apartment. That's about all. And, I suppose, she led a somewhat…individual kind of life…"

"And you think Leonard knew her?" she asked curiously. "Why?"

He was in water deeper than he'd anticipated. He shook his head. "None…really. It just came out. I don't know what made me say it."

She observed him for a moment, unconvinced. Then she shook her head. "I can't see Leonard Channing getting involved with a whore. If that's what she was."

"I shouldn't have said it," Eric admitted.

"Least of all to Hallam." She glanced across to the businessman, helping himself from the brandy decanter. She half-whispered to Eric, "That man can really be boorish, can't he? Such a difference between him and Dato' Rashid."

Or Jason Sullivan, QC, Eric considered.

Almost as though she had guessed his thoughts, Anne said, "You've barely spoken to Jason tonight."

He looked at her levelly. "Neither have you."

Her glance dropped after a moment. "I've been in his company quite enough in Singapore," she said carelessly. "But he is a guest, and I think you should be more than just barely polite."

Eric inclined his head ironically, in a slight bow. "I'll dance attendance immediately."

"Eric—"

"Yes?"

There was an odd expression in her eyes: an amalgam of anxiety and anger. "What's the matter with you? I don't know what it is, but you seem withdrawn tonight, and…I feel almost as though I don't know you any more. You're different. There's some kind of distance growing between us."

He regarded her soberly. "I didn't think that was just tonight."

She twirled her half-full brandy glass between her fingers, glancing around the room. Sullivan was talking animatedly to

Dato' Rashid, Hallam had joined the Lord Lieutenant again, along with the two other makeweights Anne had invited. "We've got to *talk*," she said suddenly, in a fierce, lowered tone. "We've got to get some answers."

"Provided we get the questions right," he replied quietly.

She looked at him briefly, her eyes dancing with anger, then turned on her heel, walked across the room and slipped her hand into the crook of Jason Sullivan's arm. Eric watched her for a few moments, as she laughed, looked up to Sullivan and flirted openly with him. The barrister seemed surprised, glanced up towards Eric for a moment and then grinned down at her, responded with animation. Eric put down his glass and walked across the room to the large French windows that led out onto the terrace.

He opened the windows and stepped through into the darkness of the evening. The wind had dropped; the air was still and cold to his hot cheek. He looked about him, at the dimly seen slopes of the hill outlined against the night sky, the glitter and dance of winter stars above his head, sharp as the frost that would probably come by morning. He had enjoyed these last ten years at Sedleigh Hall—and though he was committed to his miserable practice in Newcastle, dealing with the grubby underbelly of Tyneside life, he yet appreciated that returning to Sedleigh, and the country air, was a necessary antidote, a balance that made his life not only bearable, but exhilarating.

But now there was a tension here, and he could not focus on it, because he was afraid of what the answers might be, if he asked the necessary questions.

He was aware that someone was joining him, stepping out onto the terrace. He turned. It was Dato' Rashid: suave, elegant, breathing deeply at the sharp air. He smiled at Eric; behind him, Joe Hallam also moved to stand in the doorway, tall, heavy, solid. Yet there was a tension about him, an uncertainty in his body language.

Rashid looked about him, stepping closer to Eric. "The temperature, it is so different from my country. There, every day and every evening is the same—around twenty-eight degrees. The regular thunderstorms cool the air, of course, but it is only rarely we see stars such as are here in your Western skies. And we never experience this cold." He shivered, theatrically. "But one should experience all things, don't you agree? Without experience, how can one learn?" He pushed his hands deep into the pockets of his dinner jacket. "I was talking to Mr Hallam back there, a little while ago. He tells me you have been working together, on a take over of a company on Tyneside. Has it experienced difficulties?"

Eric was aware of Hallam stepping forward onto the terrace. He seemed to be uneasy about something, as though eager to hear Eric's reply.

It never came.

Hallam was outlined, stepping forward through the French windows onto the terrace; Dato' Rashid was at Eric's elbow, a few feet in front of Hallam; Eric was half turning, about to speak. The noise came like a crack, a snapping sound on the night air. Eric was aware of a waspish hum, and then the echo of the rifle seemed to boom towards the distant fell, an obscene sound sharp in the winter sky.

Hallam gasped. Dato' Rashid had staggered, pushed back against him, out of control, unbalanced. Then the Malaysian businessman fell to the flagged terrace. His dark eyes were wide, staring in shock, and he seemed to be trying to say something, but it was in a language other than English. Eric plunged forward, reaching out a hand as the Malaysian collapsed on the terrace.

It was when he knelt over him that he saw the slow, dark seeping of blood staining the man's white shirt front. There was a stunned, frozen silence and then Rashid gasped, gave a slow moaning sigh, and then there was a rattling in his throat, the bubbling of bloody froth on his lips. As Eric knelt beside him he fell silent, his eyes staring blankly at the cold glittering stars, indifferent in the winter sky.

3

The headlights of the Jaguar lanced along the road in front of him: he had left way behind him the narrow lanes leading from

Sedleigh Hall and he was now able to unleash the full power of the car as he careered down the A1, heading back towards Newcastle, and the river.

It had been chaos back at the hall. They had lifted Rashid back into the dining room: he was shivering violently when he regained consciousness, but was still barely able to speak, his eyes wide, roaming as though seeking something, glaring in their panic. The Lord Lieutenant had showed decisiveness for once—perhaps he was used to crisis or had been trained to manage it in his old Army days. He called the ambulance services, and the police. His tones were clipped, his manner efficient.

The others milled about uncertainly, shocked, some peering nervously through the windows out to the darkness of the hill. Jason Sullivan seemed to be totally floored: his face was white, his handsome features drawn, but Eric noted that it was he who attempted to calm Anne, one arm across her shoulders as she stared in disbelief at her stricken guest. She seemed dazed with incomprehension, unable to come to terms with the situation.

Eric stepped to the windows and glanced out, not really expecting to see anything beyond the terrace, then he closed the windows. Anger thundered through his veins: he felt his home had been invaded and an unreasoning fury devoured him. He was at a loss to explain how the attack upon Rashid had come about—he could not imagine any reason for it and yet somehow it seemed to be almost symptomatic of the disorder in which his life seemed to have been immersed of late. He had behaved uncharacteristically, he had strayed away from his principles, his personal life was threatened, and his professional future lay in the hands of a police officer he neither liked nor trusted. And he was no closer to reaching a conclusion, or a solution to the problems that beset him.

But this new situation enraged him, denying him the capacity for rational thought.

Rashid was trying to say something.

His dark eyes were on Eric, standing over him: there was almost a pleading took about his glance, edged with anxiety, a draining panic. Eric stooped over him, knelt beside him, strained to catch what the man was trying to say. The lips were blood-flecked, the tongue thick inside the mouth. But after a moment, Eric understood what the man was saying.

"Hallam..."

Eric stared at him for a few moments, frowned and then shook his head in uncertainty. He stood up, understanding nothing, and looked about him. There was no sign of the Newcastle businessman: the rest of the dinner party still milled around like anxious sheep, one or two still with glasses in their hands. Eric walked across to Anne, standing beside the comforting Jason Sullivan.

"Have you seen Hallam?" Eric asked shortly. "Rashid wants him for some reason."

Anne shook her head dumbly. She still seemed shattered by the events that now swirled around her in the confines of her own home. Jason Sullivan jerked his head towards the door. "I think I saw him head out there, towards the hall. Shortly after we brought Rashid into the room. Is...is he going to be all right?"

"Rashid?" Eric shrugged. This was probably the first time Sullivan had been face to face personally with an act of violence: barristers dealt with the consequences of violence in the courtroom, not the realities of the moment. Eric's experience was different. He'd been here before—in the back streets of Newcastle, on the moors, and along the river. "It's a chest wound. Much will depend on how quickly the medics get here."

"What does he want with Hallam?" Anne managed to ask. Her eyes were glazed, her hands trembling slightly.

"I don't know." Eric glanced around him towards the doorway, then left Anne with Sullivan and walked out into the hall. He hesitated, then stepped out to the main drive at the front of the house. The cars were clustered there, waiting for their occupants. Apart from one: there was a space where Hallam's car had been parked. He had not stopped to await the arrival of the police.

A quick dizziness suddenly swept over Eric: it was succeeded by a tumbling of questions in his mind, darts of anxiety seeking attention. Seemingly dissociated events crowded into his head.

He found himself thinking about Hallam, the pressure that he seemed to have been under, trying to rush the meeting with the owners of Barker Marine. Then there was Leonard Channing: Eric recalled the way in which his questioning of Channing might have provoked the heart attack, even though the man had clearly been ill already. Pressure…suddenly he could see again the fragment of the fax sheet clearly in his mind, and he thought of Hallam's nervousness on the terrace, standing near to Rashid, just before the bullet had come slamming out of the darkness. And now there was Hallam's disappearance. It was as though he was running from something…

And sharply, vividly, at the forefront of his mind once more was the frozen, shattering image of the body of Sandra Vitali sprawled lifeless just inside her own front door. The link was there, somehow…Eric turned abruptly, went back inside. He stood there glaring at the scene, the huddled, distraught guests, the man breathing agonizingly from the wound in his chest, Anne's white face. He stepped forward. Still gripped with indecision, he yet felt the need to do something. He could not simply stand there, wait around. Harshly, he said, "I've got to go out."

"What? Where?" she asked, confused.

"The ambulance should get here fairly soon. And the police won't be long."

She put out a hand to detain him, but he ignored her, turned, hurried away. He grabbed the car keys from the library table, almost ran out to the Jaguar. When he glanced back, rolling the car out of the drive, he caught a glimpse of Jason Sullivan waving at the steps, shouting something, but he ignored him, drove out into the dark, tree-shrouded lanes, and gunned his way south.

Two miles from the house he saw the blue light flashing on a distant rise, and he slowed, pulled in to one side. A few moments later an ambulance swept past him, headed for Sedleigh Hall. A half mile behind it was a police car. It sped past him, barely aware of his presence.

When they had passed, Eric continued on his way. He had no idea what he was hoping to find, but there was a cold feeling in his chest as he thought over the events of the last days. It was only instinct, but he had an overwhelming gut feeling that the answer might well lie at Tyneside.

On board the *Lady Ghislaine.*

He rolled the Jaguar over the last two hundred yards, almost silently, with his lights off, until he reached the edge of the bluff overlooking the boatyard and the *Lady Ghislaine* at her moorings. He stepped out of the car carefully, closing the door with a light click, and walked forward until he had a clear view of the seagoing yacht below. The scene was different from the last time he had been here: there was no light in the security guard's hut, and the fenced entrance to the boatyard hung open. A car was parked inside the yard. Eric stared at it: Joe Hallam had arrived at Sedleigh Hall in a black Porsche. The outlines of the car parked close to the *Lady Ghislaine* were vague in the dim light, but it was Eric's guess that the car was Hallam's.

From where he was standing he could see a chink of light emerging past the curtains of the main stateroom; a moment later, as he watched, a glow appeared in the pilot house. He hesitated, was about to start making his way down the bluff to the yard when he caught sight of a movement below him, at the foot of the bluff, in the dark roadway alongside the fence. It seemed that someone else was arriving at the berth of the *Lady Ghislaine,* someone who was showing the same kind of wariness displayed by Eric Ward. The dark shape of the car had come to a stop, lights dimmed, just fifty yards from the boatyard, and the man who emerged walked with care. He was headed straight for the *Lady Ghislaine.*

From the bluff, Eric watched as the newcomer slipped stealthily towards the yacht, keeping in the shadows, moving silently and carefully. He could make out little about the man, except that he wore dark clothing, kept his head low. But he was clearly intent on boarding the boat: as Eric watched, he saw the man enter the gateway, slip across the yard, and reach the aft ladder; a moment later he was stepping soundlessly onto the aft deck, and then he was lost to sight.

Eric waited uncertainly for a few moments. He shook his head: he had come this far, and there was no turning back now. He took a deep breath, and started down the slope.

The moonlight was pale and fitful: dark clouds rolled at a funereal pace across the sky, shrouding the river, cloaking its dark waters, lending an air of danger and mystery to the barely seen shorelines. As Eric clambered down the slope his mind was in a whirl: he was beginning to sense some kind of pattern, some kind of logic in the strands of information he had gained over the last few days. He was certain that there was some kind of link between Leonard Channing and Sandra Vitali; the murders of Vitali and Sam Cullen were now being attributed by the police to Mad Jack Tenby's enforcer Terry Morton, the man Eric had glimpsed at the dead woman's apartment block; and there was a link between Hallam and Channing. As for Rashid…it suddenly occurred to Eric that maybe the bullet that had struck down the Malaysian businessman had not in fact been meant for him at all—the real target had been Joe Hallam, standing close by.

But why was Hallam being stalked with a view to a kill? And by whom? Eric's guess at a solution to the first question was hazy, but he harboured the suspicion that the man who had just climbed aboard the *Lady Ghislaine* was Terry Morton. The man had already killed Sandra Vitali and Sam Cullen—and now it seemed that Hallam was the target in view.

Terry Morton…or perhaps Charlie Spate had been right, and Mad Jack Tenby was at last showing his hand.

He had reached the yard entrance: he glanced at the lock, and saw it had been left dangling from the fence. He looked around towards the darkened security hut and reasoned that Hallam must have told the security guard he was free to leave, before he had parked in the yard and gone aboard the *Lady Ghislaine.*

Quietly Eric moved across the yard, hesitated at the foot of the ladder leading to the aft deck. As he stood there, there was a deep rumbling sound, and he heard someone leaving the pilot house. He pressed against the hull of the boat, hidden in the shadows as Joe Hallam came out on the deck. He was still in his dinner jacket: Eric caught the flash of pale moonlight on his white shirt-front as the man leaned forward, casting off at the bow. Then he came walking along the deck, to cast off astern.

Joe Hallam was leaving the river—and Eric's guess was now confirmed. It was Hallam who owned the *Lady Ghislaine*, under cover of the name EMF Enterprises. And it had been Hallam whom Leonard Channing had contacted in the boat's soundproofed office.

White water began to churn behind Eric: he had no idea what had happened to Morton, but he knew the man was on board, and unthinkingly Eric stepped quickly up the ladder as Hallam moved back into the pilot house, ready to take the wheel, and thunder the engines into an escape from the river.

He crouched down behind the window aft, that looked into the main stateroom: there was still a gleam of light there, but the windows were heavily curtained. Eric moved forward quietly, began to climb the steps up to the deck behind the pilot house and a moment later froze, as he caught sight of the back of Joe Hallam's head, standing at the wheel, the extended deck of electronic devices winking greenly, haloing him in an eerie light.

But even as Eric hesitated, he saw the shadow move behind Hallam, the hand reaching out, the muzzle of the pistol placed firmly just behind Hallam's right ear, and everything seemed to stand still, the stunned tableau in the pilot house unmoving, unyielding as panic stiffened Hallam into immobility.

Eric heard Hallam's gasp in the cold night air. "What..."

"Carefully, my friend, carefully." The intruder's voice was cool, but there was a viciousness underlying it. "Just shut down the engines, and step away from the wheel."

There was a long moment of stillness and then Hallam's shaking hand went to the controls, the deep throatiness of the engines was muted to a subdued rumbling, and the churning of white water aft slowed.

Hallam did not turn his head, but he knew the man he was dealing with. "It...it wasn't my doing, believe me!" Hallam gasped, staring straight ahead, the gun muzzle still pressed against his skull.

"Of course not," the gunman soothed. "None of it was ever your doing."

"But it's true!" Hallam pleaded urgently. "I was doing my job, that's all! I never wanted to get involved in the other side of things!"

"But you always *were* involved," the intruder gritted. "You were organizing the purchase of Barker Marine. Don't tell me you never realized the reason behind the purchase."

"I thought—"

"Thought? You knew, dammit. Don't play the innocent with me! Once Barker Marine were out of the way the plan was always to develop a secure deep-water anchorage so that boats like this damned motor yacht could come in, ostensibly as pleasure craft, but bringing in drugs, right into the heart of Tyneside!"

"I swear—"

"You swear you didn't know it was all part of the same trade?" The man with the gun laughed, an unpleasant, harsh sound. "Don't expect me to believe you were so naive."

"But...but you've hit him now. You've killed him." There was the quaver of fear in Hallam's voice. "What...what do you want with me?"

There was a short silence. When the reply came it was delivered in almost a dreamy tone. "Revenge, I suppose. And the closing of a book. Now step away from the wheel."

"But I wasn't *involved,* I swear it. What are you going to do?" Hallam was panic-stricken. He turned his head slightly, against the gun.

"I told you. Even up scores. Now step back away...easy, now. We're going down into the main stateroom, Hallam, so just step gently, and carefully...I don't want to spread what brains you have all over the deck..."

Eric shrank back against the bulkhead, ducking his head as the men in the pilot house turned in his direction. He heard Hallam's unsteady, stumbling progress across the deck, the gunman silent-footed behind him then the clambering down the ladder as they both went down into the stateroom. As soon as they were out of sight Eric moved silently up the ladder and entered the pilot house. He stood there for a moment, irresolute, as he heard Hallam's whining tone below.

"Why...what do you want me down here for?"

The man with the gun was chuckling, unpleasantly. "Well, you were all set to run after I downed Rashid. You must have known I'd be after you next. And it was a good idea, heading for the *Lady Ghislaine*—except I guessed that would be the way a rat like you would run for cover. Anyway, it suited me. So I watched you run from Sedleigh Hall, and I just made my own way here, knowing you'd get everything started for me, engine warmed up, lines cast off..."

"All right," Hallam interrupted urgently. "Take the boat—get the hell out of here. If the police find their way to me, I'll tell them I know nothing about why Rashid was killed. I..."

"You can be relied upon, I know," the intruder said sarcastically. "To do just what Rashid told you. To kill Sandra—"

"Look, I had no *choice*," Hallam pleaded desperately. "I never wanted any part of this business. I had no idea Rashid would ever want anything from me other than to front his legitimate business enterprises. The EMF company was into importing Malaysian timber, I thought the Shoreline company was going to be involved in that—"

"That's crap, Hallam," the gunman said evenly.

"I swear it! And I told him there'd be trouble when he contacted me, said there were a couple of jobs he needed me to do..."

"Like killing Sandra?" The gunman's voice turned to a sneer. "And killing Sam Cullen in his own apartment?"

"What could I do? I didn't know what a malicious bastard Rashid could be!"

Eric was sweating. He was standing on the second step of the ladder in the hatchway. Below him, he recalled, was the short corridor, then to the right the narrow vestibule leading into the main stateroom. Silently, the blood thundering in his head, he moved down the stairs into the darkened corridor. Light streamed from the stateroom; thrown across the corridor he could see the shadow of the gunman, standing in the doorway, threatening Hallam within.

"Anyway, enough talk. It's all over, now, the whole business. Rashid's gone—"

"What are you going to do to me here?" Hallam's terrified voice rose an octave as he stared down the barrel of the pistol.

"I'm going to give you what you deserve. It's better down here—I'd not be comfortable with your blood in the pilot house. I'm sailing out of this damned river, Hallam, and it'll never see me again. I've got things arranged in Spain, and from there, probably South America. I've still got money stashed away, and I've still got contacts. And with Rashid out of the way..."

"But I can help you! I can give you the kind of support that I gave Rashid!"

"The only thing I want from you is silence. I'm away from the Tyne, but so are you. It was a bad mistake on your part, doing Rashid's bidding. And now you're going to pay for it. You'll be fish food in the North Sea while I'm heading south."

"This is crazy! It's not necessary! I swear to you..."

It was a vain plea. Eric saw the shadow of the man's arm rise, knew the finger was tightening on the trigger. He tensed, poised to step around into the vestibule and hurl himself at the gunman. He heard Joe Hallam's voice crack as he pleaded, again, desperately.

"But it wasn't my doing...I just followed Rashid's orders! I had no choice! For God's sake, don't do this, Cullen!"

Cullen.

The name jolted Eric like a blow in the stomach, but he was already moving. He stepped into the vestibule, saw the shadow half-turning, aware of his presence, and then he launched himself at the man with the gun.

4

The sound of the gunshot in the enclosed surroundings of the stateroom was explosive. Eric cannoned into the gunman, and the shot went wildly into the ceiling. Next moment he was down, rolling on the thickly carpeted deck of the stateroom, grappling with the strong, twisting body below him. He caught a glimpse of Cullen's face: it was puffed and bruised, swollen, a redly new scar slashed across his forehead, and as they rolled, Eric struggling to grip the gun hand, he realized that the man who had died in Cullen's apartment had been the enforcer who had come to kill him. There had been a fight to the death on that occasion between Terry Morton and Sam Cullen—but now it was Eric who was struggling to stay alive.

Cullen was strong: his face was contorted with fury and effort, but Eric had his wrist in a vice-like grip. Even so, he was straining to hold him as they writhed, gasping for breath, struggling for the upper hand. A chair went over with a crash, and Eric caught a glimpse of Joe Hallam, white-faced with shock at Eric's entrance, still recovering his nerve.

Eric was weakening: the hard, muscular body underneath him was twisting, pushing upwards: Eric had locked his legs against Cullen's, forcing him to the carpeted deck but slowly the man was rising against him, teeth gritted with effort, bruised features contorted, eyes glaring, and the gun hand was coming up, inexorably.

"Hallam!" Eric shouted, but the man seemed paralysed, his courage gone in the panic of the last few minutes. Then in a sudden surge, Cullen's elbow came up, breaking free, and his forearm struck Eric across the throat in a violent blow. Eric fell sideways, choking. He rolled, gagging, and Cullen was free of him. The man was rising, his face twisted with rage; he was on his knees, glaring at Eric and the gun hand was coming up, the pistol pointing directly at Eric's head.

Hallam moved at last.

As Eric lay there, it seemed to him that it occurred almost in a slow-motion dream. Hallam came up behind Cullen and kicked at him: the toe of Hallam's shoe connected with Cullen's ear and the man was thrown sideways, cannoning against the corner of the table. Hallam swore, kicked at him again but the blow took Cullen on the shoulder. He groaned, tried to lift the gun again but Hallam's brief surge of courage had already left him and he was running for the corridor, jumping over the prostrate, half-dazed form of the man who had come to kill him, heading for the stairs and the hatchway.

He never made it. The gun was wavering, and Cullen's blood-shot eyes were glazed but the bullet took Hallam in the back as he was outlined in the doorway. It slammed him forward: he hit the far wall of the narrow corridor, seemed to stand there for a long moment, fingers scrabbling at the wall as though desperate for purchase, and then he fell backwards, back into the state-room lurching, coughing, collapsing only feet from where Eric lay.

Cullen was barely conscious. He was staring at Eric, and the gun was still up, but the muzzle was wavering, uncertain. The kick to the head had dazed him; the collision with the table had further drained his senses and he seemed unable to focus. His swollen, bruised mouth was working spasmodically, his breathing irregular, and a slow seepage of blood coursed from under his short-cropped hair and across his forehead. Still choking and gasping for breath, Eric made one last effort. He rolled, half rising again, and even as determination gleamed once more in Cullen's crazed eyes and the gun muzzle swung, following Eric's progress, Eric hit him. His elbow slammed into Cullen's temple, his forearm crashing against Cullen's nose. There was the snapping sound of breaking bone and the man slumped sideways, the breath expelled from him in a gasp. The gun dropped from fingers that were suddenly nerveless, and blood gushed freely from his nostrils.

Eric lay there beside his unconscious assailant for what seemed an age. His own breath was uncontrolled; he was gasping, retching as he fought to clear his airways, drag oxygen into his lungs. There was no sound from Hallam: Eric guessed Cullen had achieved what he had set out to do. But he had no energy to check: his throat was constricted, his lungs heaving, and the old, familiar scratching of cat claws had begun again, at the back of his eyes.

It was several minutes before he was able to reach across, pull the gun from Cullen's hand. The man's eyes were closed, but he was still breathing, and the beaten features were marked with slow blood, from his temple, and from his nose. There was no urgency now. Eric slowly sat up, still gasping, the pain behind his eyes becoming almost unbearable.

Almost thirty minutes had passed before he was able, half blind, to crawl towards the soundproofed office, and use the phone.

Charlie Spate stood stiffly, not quite to attention, in front of the Chief Constable, the early morning winter sun gleaming on the highly polished desk. He waited: he had been called to the office, but the Chief Constable was disinclined to acknowledge his presence immediately. He was a busy man: things had to be fitted into place in proper time, and he was now inspecting the file in front of him, his greying head nodding slightly, not entirely approving, but partly satisfied. That was something, at least, Spate thought grimly.

"Right bloody mess, wasn't it, Spate?"

"I suppose you could say that, sir."

"I just did," the Chief Constable replied, raising his head and observing the detective inspector with a certain equanimity. "It looks as though you were barking up the wrong tree all along."

"Not entirely, sir," Spate said, miffed.

"You insisted Jack Tenby was behind all this," the Chief Constable observed, with a degree of malicious pleasure. "Wanting to turn back the clock, take control of drugs on Tyneside."

"Well..."

"Whereas..." The Chief Constable put the tips of his fingers together, inspected them, admired the neatly manicured nails. "Well, let's hear your explanation. What'll be appearing in your report, when you make it?"

Charlie Spate cleared his throat. "Hallam's killing leaves us with a certain problem, because I'm pretty sure we'd have got the full story from him. But I think we can piece most of it together, and nail Sam Cullen completely. It seems that it all centres around the Malaysian, Rashid bin Abdullah."

"Ah, yes..." The Chief Constable's eyes were hooded reflectively.

"While he's still recovering in hospital, representations of a diplomatic kind have already been made about him. It seems he's rather well connected back home. They want him back."

"I don't see how we can let that save him," Spate insisted. "He may well have contacts, and know the right people in Malaysia, but according to the information we now have it's Dato' Rashid who's been responsible for the supply of a considerable part of the drug trade here on Tyneside."

"Through Sam Cullen."

"That's right, sir. The way of it was that Cullen worked for Rashid. The Malaysian financed him, set him up in business: he has a big operation. I think once Interpol look into it we'll find Rashid's tentacles have spread into Europe in a big way. But Cullen, he was Rashid's local organizer along the Tyne."

"And Hallam?"

Charlie Spate shook his head. "Rashid kept his businesses in separate compartments. Hallam wasn't really involved directly in the drug-running—his was a separate deal with Rashid. He was the front man to pursue legitimate business interests, although it included the purchase of a site along the river to give Rashid a more secure base for the drug operations."

"While Cullen actually ran the drugs...But Cullen got greedy?"

"That's about the size of it," Spate agreed, nodding his head. "Cullen decided he could set up his own contacts, run his own operations. He'd used Sandra Vitali as a mule—though that wasn't her only talent—and she'd helped make connections for him in Asia. It seems they had a thing going, too...you know, sexual. But when Cullen pulled Sandra out of the runs, and then let it be known through a courier—the man who was found dead in KLIA—that he was splitting away to set up his own thing on Tyneside, that wasn't something Rashid was prepared to tolerate. If he allowed Tyneside to be taken over, where else would he be cut out? So he put the word out. Sandra Vitali and Sam Cullen were to be eliminated. As an example."

"*Pour encourager les autres,*" the Chief Constable mused. "And the word went to...?"

"Joe Hallam," Spate said grimly. "I don't think Hallam was very pleased about it all: he didn't want to get too closely involved in the drug operation. But he was in too deep in other ways. When I mentioned that the Vitali woman had other talents, the fact is she was known to Hallam as well as Cullen. She was a call girl in London when Hallam first met her…he used her services from time to time, favours to valued customers, clients and friends. I gather that sort of came back to the forefront when she pulled out of the courier business in Asia. She thought things were getting too hot for her."

He scratched his nose thoughtfully. "Of course, Hallam wasn't going to do the hits himself. He recruited Terry Morton for that—Mad Jack Tenby's enforcer."

He saw the Chief Constable bridle at the name. "Ex-enforcer, so Mr Tenby assures us."

"That's as may be. Anyway, it seems Morton hoped to deal with Vitali in the hotel car park, but was forced eventually to do the job in her apartment. She came to the door, maybe expecting someone else, and it was easy—Morton stepped inside, broke her neck. But when he went to deal with Cullen it was a different story. He found himself in a battle. Cullen was tough. He took a hell of a beating, but he managed to get the better of Morton."

"So the man whom your witness…Stevens?"

"That's right, sir."

"The man he saw carrying a body, and who knocked him down the stairs, that was actually Cullen?"

"Yes, sir." Spate paused, reflectively. "We'd have found out sooner, if the labs had got their act together. Anyway, we've had the forensic report on that corpse from the headland now: it's Morton all right. Cullen killed him, dumped him on the cliffs, burned out the car…"

"Why go to that trouble?"

"Cullen wanted to slow things down, make people think it was he who'd been killed. While he waited for Rashid to show on Tyneside. His Asian sources had told him that the Malaysian was coming over on business. Cullen planned to get his revenge."

"He almost did," the Chief Constable said thoughtfully. "But the bullet didn't kill Rashid."

"The next one certainly killed Hallam. Anyway, we have the rifle—it was still in Cullen's car—and we have the gun that killed Hallam."

"Hmm..." The Chief Constable was silent for a while. "So we have Cullen, and can pin the murder of Terry Morton and Hallam on him; and we have Rashid, with Cullen giving evidence that it was Rashid who ordered the killing of Sandra Vitali."

"It's the only reason why Cullen is talking," Spate said. "He failed to get Rashid, so this way he can still get his revenge—even if it also costs him. But we got him bang to rights anyway, over the killing of Hallam. After all, Eric Ward is an eyewitness."

The Chief Constable nodded slowly. "Where exactly do we fit *him* in?"

Charlie Spate hesitated. He'd been thinking about this for some time. He shrugged, reluctantly. "It seems...it seems after Rashid was downed, Hallam fled. He guessed he'd be next. Ward was suspicious: when he saw Hallam do a runner, he followed him, to the *Lady Ghislaine*. The boat was owned by a Rashid–Hallam company, EMF Enterprises. Hallam ran for it; Ward followed him. It was just a lucky chance," he lied lamely.

The Chief Constable seemed unconvinced. He sniffed. "Maybe so, maybe so. All right, get it all written up and we'll set the necessary wheels in motion." He paused, a gleam of malice in his eyes. "By the way, Mr Tenby came in to see me yesterday."

"Yes, sir?"

"He was...er...pleased to hear we've accepted he wasn't involved in all this business. And he also offered some...advice on another matter. The Gilsland burglary."

"Is that so?"

"We have a name now, other than the man you've been questioning. Stevens, isn't it? The man who was also present when Cullen emerged with Morton's body. Well, Mr Tenby has given us a lead—it seems we were in...error over Stevens. We have Mr Tenby to thank for getting it right."

"Very public-spirited of Mr Tenby." Charlie Spate made no attempt to keep the sarcasm out of his voice. He could guess why Tenby had volunteered the information. Rattled over the accusations, and worried about his newly developed position of respectability, he had decided to give the police a name, even if it meant the release of a man who owed him money. But he let the Chief Constable have his little triumph. There'd be other days, he considered as he was dismissed from the presence, some other opportunity to put the screws on Mad Jack Tenby.

When he returned to his own office Elaine Start was there. She raised an eyebrow. "You heard we've got a tearaway for the Gilsland burglary?"

"The Chief just told me," Spate grunted. He shook his head. "That's Tenby, trying to clean the slate, keep in with the top brass and his new friends in their manor houses. It's called upward mobility." He thought for a moment. "You…er…you got that file containing the written statement from Eric Ward?"

She nodded. He watched as she walked across to the locked filing cabinet and retrieved the brown manila folder. He liked the way she moved. She really did have a good figure. When she handed him the folder, he asked, "You've kept this under wraps, like I said."

"Of course, sir." She was watching him carefully.

"Hmm…" He opened the folder, read Ward's statement again. He was silent for a little while, thinking. "That Wister character you told me about…fiction writer, is that so?"

"Yes, sir."

"This statement…it seems to me this reads pretty much like fiction, too." He raised his eyes, stared at her pointedly for a few moments. "I don't think we need it. Doesn't assist our case against Cullen, particularly, or against Rashid. No point in letting this stuff loose on the public."

She was staring at him, appraisingly. There was a certain surprise in her eyes. Slowly, he extracted the statement, slipped it inside his jacket pocket and handed the empty file back to her. "I think we can consign this to the rubbish bin," he suggested.

She had a half-smile on her face. She thought she had detected a weakness in Charlie Spate, a reluctance to allow the name of an essentially innocent party to be dragged through the mud. She seemed to be offering Charlie a degree of grudging respect;

maybe she was even beginning to like him, think he was more human than she had supposed. But that's where women often got it wrong, Charlie thought to himself. Sure, there was no point in dragging Eric Ward's conduct into the Vitali killing. But he wasn't dumping the statement out of regard for the ex-policeman turned lawyer. Charlie Spate believed in favours: you did one, you called one in. And there might be some time in the future when he might need a favour from Eric Ward, a lawyer who knew the back streets of Newcastle, the dark stretches of the Tyne, Charlie Spate's new stamping ground.

And when that happened, Charlie could call in the debt.

5

Eric had taken the call from Tramline Stevens that morning. Stevens had been effusive in his praise and thanks. Even though Eric had denied he'd done anything to help get the man off the Gilsland charge, his client was not persuaded. "They've got the young tearaway who done it," Stevens announced. "So I'm in the clear."

"Except in respect of your debt with Tenby."

"Ah, I got plans about that. There's a horse running in the third at Newcastle today. It's a walkover. I'll be able to pay off Mad Jack and there's an end to it..."

Eric doubted that. There would never be an end to it for Tramline Stevens.

But he dismissed the man from his mind: he was still thinking about the conversation he'd had with Anne the previous evening. Inevitably, she had been sceptical about his story of having followed Hallam's car to the *Lady Ghislaine*. But she did not pursue things too much: she clearly had other things on her mind.

"This business over Rashid," she said bitterly, "it's going to cause problems over our Singapore deal. Rashid's influence was crucial. Jason feels that in the circumstances we'd be well advised to pull out now, cut our losses, lick our wounds."

"I think he's right," Eric said levelly. "Besides, maybe there's a better investment you could make with your money."

"Such as?" she queried, frowning.

"Barker Marine. They're in bad trouble—and the takeover by Rashid's front company, Shoreline Investments, that's come crashing down too in the circumstances. You could do a deal with them: build the company up again with new finance, save a few jobs on Tyneside."

She eyed him thoughtfully. "I'll think about that. Maybe have a word with Jason about it."

"I'd do that. At the same time," Eric added, "talk to him about replacing me and representing your interests on the board of Martin and Channing."

She was silent for a while, fiddling with the ring on her finger. "You never liked working with Leonard Channing, did you?"

"No, I didn't. But that's irrelevant: I don't think he'll be active in the bank again. It's just that, as far as I'm concerned, I think it's time for a change."

"And you think Jason might be the best man to act for me?"

"Don't you?"

Suddenly the question was there between them, not the one he had asked, but the one that had remained unspoken for some time. It was about the tension that lay between them, what might or might not have happened in Singapore, her relationship with Jason Sullivan, the nature and strength of their marriage. Her eyes were fixed on his. Quietly, she said, "What is it you want to know, Eric?"

He shrugged carelessly, saying nothing, but feeling a slow ache in his chest.

She sighed. "Leonard Channing...I went to see him yesterday. He's recovering slowly. But there's a rumour...it's being said that he had some link with that murdered woman. Sandra Vitali."

Eric's mouth was dry. He made no response. He knew now that Hallam had introduced Channing to Sandra, that it was Channing she had probably been expecting to meet that evening she had died, Hallam's favour, providing a call-girl for a business partner on his trip to the north-east. Not that Channing would have been allowed to take her home, not with Terry Morton lurking in the car park. But if he were to share such thoughts with Anne it could lead to other matters, other disclosures.

"There *are* questions, aren't there?" she asked. Her chin came up defiantly. "But I'm not sure they should be asked. You could ask me whether anything happened between me and Jason in Singapore. And...and I could ask you whether you were telling me the truth when you told me you didn't know Sandra Vitali."

The silence grew between them, heavy, uneasy. At last she shook her head. "Maybe the answers would satisfy each of us; maybe they'd hurt, leave wounds. Perhaps the questions are best buried, unasked."

His voice was slightly shaky. "Someone once wrote, somewhere, that every answer is a form of death."

"Yes," she said slowly. "A form of death. Maybe that's right." She took a deep breath and held his glance. "So why don't we just leave things like that? And try to start again."

Why not, he thought dully. But he was not certain, perhaps he would never be certain that it was the right thing to do. One day, perhaps, he would know.

But not right now.